"I don't need your protection."

Hurt flickered in his gaze then vanished behind a stone cold stare. *Oh...I didn't mean to say that.* She hadn't meant to hurt him. When would it ever end?

Her legs trembled with fear and her lips weren't far behind. She wouldn't let him see her like this—though why she wanted to hide that from him she wasn't sure. After all, someone was trying to kill them and she *was* scared. But she didn't want him to protect her. She didn't want to be that vulnerable.

Did she have a choice?

And wasn't Zach scared too? Trying to read his mind, sense his emotional state, wouldn't do either of them any good. Again, she averted her gaze, listening, watching for the shooters as she caught her breath.

Zach gently touched her chin and turned her to face him. "Are you okay?"

It hurt when he touched her like that, all gentle and caring. She didn't want that from him, or for him to see that she was absolutely not okay.

Elizabeth Goddard is the award-winning author of more than thirty novels and novellas. A 2011 Carol Award winner, she's a double finalist in the 2016 Daphne du Maurier Award for Excellence in Mystery/Suspense, and a 2016 Carol Award finalist. Elizabeth graduated with a computer science degree and worked in high-level software sales before retiring to write full-time.

Books by Elizabeth Goddard

Love Inspired Suspense

Wilderness, Inc.

Targeted for Murder
Undercover Protector
False Security

Mountain Cove

Buried
Untraceable
Backfire
Submerged
Tailspin
Deception

Freezing Point
Treacherous Skies
Riptide
Wilderness Peril

Visit the Author Profile page at Harlequin.com.

FALSE SECURITY

ELIZABETH GODDARD

HARLEQUIN® LOVE INSPIRED® SUSPENSE

Recycling programs for this product may not exist in your area.

ISBN-13: 978-0-373-45700-7

False Security

This edition published by arrangement with Love Inspired Books.

www.Harlequin.com

Printed in U.S.A.

Be still, and know that I am God; I will be exalted among the nations, I will be exalted in the earth.

—*Psalms* 46:10

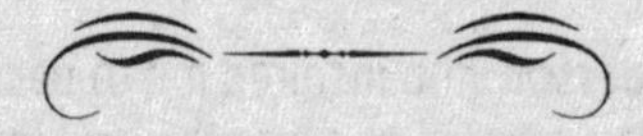

To Mom. Oh, how I miss you! But we will be together again in glory with our Lord and savior, Christ Jesus.

Acknowledgments

I've lost the person who inspired me to become an avid reader and the person who was the greatest influence on my life in this writing endeavor, but regardless, I want to thank my mother for loving me and raising me to know the Lord so that I may have the hope of seeing her again one day soon. And as always, I appreciate the encouragement I receive daily from the dear writing friends God has brought into my life, and for my awesome editor, Elizabeth Mazer, and my amazing agent, Steve Laube, who makes me feel like I'm his only client.

ONE

Siskiyou Mountains, southwest Oregon

Olivia Kendricks slowed the snowmobile as she drew near the house, flakes growing thicker by the minute, etching the roof, fireplace and window seals in white and turning her home into a cottage from a Thomas Kinkade painting. Even after two winters here, that picturesque scene always filled her with peace.

Except today. Instead of that sense of peace, an eerie feeling crept over her.

Olivia continued forward. Traveling by snowmobile provided the best way to get here in the winter, unless she wanted to plow the long, curvy drive up the mountain when several feet of the white stuff buried the road. And she didn't. Besides, Olivia enjoyed the ride.

She lived for it.

The whine of the snowmobile resounded through the forest, echoing off the snow-covered trees as she steered the vehicle all the way in. She parked next to the covered garage protecting her old truck, then turned off the ignition.

Something was wrong. What was it?

Then she realized the lights were off in the house.

Strange.

She removed her helmet, shook out her hair and slid off the vehicle. Flakes accumulated in her lashes and she wiped them away as she entered the front door of the family vacation cabin where she'd taken up residence. There were no relatives left to enjoy it as a getaway anymore—well except her brother, Rich, whom she hadn't seen since their mother's funeral three years before.

That is, until yesterday.

Stomping her boots at the entrance, she hoped to disturb her brother into letting her know he was still here.

The dark house that greeted her said differently.

"Rich? Where are you?" She flicked on the lights as she made her way through the vacation-getaway-turned-cozy-home toward the room he'd slept in last night. The same room he'd used as a boy during their stays. Had he left without even saying goodbye? She hoped she'd find the few things he'd brought with him still in the room. Hoped he would stick around for a while and give them both some time to work through their issues of the past, though Rich might not be as keen to resolve them.

His backpack lay on the bed, flap hanging open and jeans and gear sprawled out. Relief swooshed through her. At least he hadn't left for good. Maybe he'd just gone out for a walk or even a snowmobile ride.

At the kitchen sink, Olivia poured a glass of water and glanced out the window, noting the snowmobile he'd ridden to the house was gone. And something…there was something in the snow.

Frowning, Olivia hurried out the back door.

Blood.

Her breath caught.

Crimson stained the snow and would soon be buried beneath a fresh layer. She let her gaze follow the path the snowmobile had taken away from the house. A trail of blood lined the tracks.

Her heart seized.

Rich!

But she couldn't let panic take hold. She had to follow that trail before the blood was hidden forever under layers of snow.

"Rich!" Olivia's gaze searched the woods even as she ran around to the front of the house for her own snowmobile.

She had to catch up to him and make sure he was okay.

Questions bombarded her as she hurried. What had happened? Why was he hurt?

Still in her snowmobile suit, she grabbed gloves and a helmet, then got back on the vehicle. Concern ratcheting up her respiration, she started the machine and sped around the house to follow in Rich's blood-spotted wake before she could no longer see the tracks. Her heart stumbled as the image of the crimson trail accosted her, but she had to focus.

Off-road and through the ungroomed woods, she'd have to be careful of hidden obstacles and fallen trees. Her eyes strained to follow the tracks and watch where she was going. His zigzagging path showed he had steered haphazardly through the woods.

"Rich!" she called through the opening in her helmet—she'd left the visor up—though she wasn't sure if he would hear her over the snowmobile.

Living this secluded in these woods, she'd traded the safety and security of knowing that she could call 911 and get a quick response for her privacy, peace and quiet.

Now she regretted that decision. She had a satellite phone that didn't work so well on cloudy days, and a radio she shared with the Wilderness, Inc. crew, but that was iffy in the mountains.

She was on her own up here for the most part.

They were on their own.

Calling his name again, she continued between the trees, grateful the thick evergreen canopy prevented the falling snow from breaking through and hiding the tracks as quickly here. At least she hadn't seen more blood, which meant that somehow he'd been able to slow the bleeding or stop it completely.

The snowmobile ground over lumps of buried boulders, and skipped along over recently fallen branches covered in fresh powder. She had to be careful that she didn't get stuck.

Why would a man who was bleeding like that get on a snowmobile and ride off into the woods?

Up ahead, Olivia spotted a snowmobile. She sped forward until she was close enough to identify it as the one Rich had used to come to the house. The snow machine was turned on its side up against a tree.

Olivia let her gaze search for any sign of Rich, fear pricking her neck like icy daggers. He could die from his injury, or he could die from hypothermia, but why had he left the house?

Had he been running from someone? Olivia wouldn't normally jump to such conclusions, except Hadley Wilde had come to this region to hide because she'd been running from an assassin and that's when she'd met and married Cooper Wilde, Wilderness, Inc. owner and Olivia's boss. Since Hadley had hidden here, it wasn't so far-fetched to think Rich had come here to hide from someone and had been attacked. It wasn't as if he'd expected to find Olivia living in the house. They hadn't spoken since their mom's funeral.

A sudden chill, much colder than the air around her, slid up her spine.

She searched the woods again for his tracks, but they were now long gone.

"Rich!" she called.

She was torn about what to do. Should she keep searching until she found him or go back for help? Either decision could be the wrong choice. She could be too late to save him either way.

God, what should I do? I can't just leave him out here. He needs help now!

Indecision twisted her insides.

Another snowmobile approached. Friend or foe? Who else would be up here besides her, Rich and whoever was the reason he'd fled the house?

Run!

Her mind screamed but her legs struggled to respond.

As the rider parked next to Rich's snowmobile, she backed away and pressed her hand against a tree trunk as though she could turn it into a weapon if needed. A knife in her pocket her only real weapon, she slipped her other hand around the hilt, wishing for the gun she'd left in her bedroom.

The rider slid from the snowmobile and pulled his visor up. Familiarity wrapped around her.

She didn't think the man was Coop or Gray, or anyone else from the Wilderness, Inc. crew. She stepped closer. "Who... Do I know you?"

But then she noticed his eyes. Those ice-blue eyes

like the color of snow in the shadows—she would never forget them.

He pulled his helmet off, his own surprise at seeing her still registering on his rugged features, his winter-wheat hair thick but mussed from the helmet.

Zachary Long.

Gone were the smooth but chiseled features of the younger man she'd known and loved. A pang shot through her. Ten years had changed him significantly. His handsome features were stronger, the sharp look of life's experiences and losses evident in his gaze, and it almost sucked the oxygen from her.

"Olivia?"

His voice wrapped around her, cradling her against the shock of seeing him. "Zach. What…what are you doing here?"

Olivia shook off the rush of emotion. "No. Scratch that. It doesn't matter. I need to find Rich. He's bleeding somewhere out there. I don't know where. The weather is turning bad and I have to find him!"

Lines creased Zach's forehead, growing deeper between his brows. He acted as if he wanted to ask questions but thought better of it and gave a subtle shake of his head.

"Let's get some help." He removed his gloves and pulled out his smartphone. "If I can't make the call, I'll try a text. Something has to go through."

Olivia wanted to laugh at that, except this was no laughing matter.

"Who could I text locally—"

Bark exploded from the tree next to her.

"Get down!" Zach hadn't been sure he could find the old Kendricks vacation place when Rich had left his cryptic and urgent message about meeting him there, but he'd been a detective in Portland long enough to know when to heed that sense something was wrong.

And he'd just gotten his confirmation.

The sound of gunfire still echoed from the shot. Zach's mind registered the danger as reflex took over.

He lunged for Olivia and threw her to the ground, pinning her under him to protect her. He remained in that position, waiting, listening.

"Why is someone shooting at us?" he whispered through the opening in her helmet, his face close to hers. This could have everything to do with Rich and his message.

"Get off me!"

Her harsh tone startled him. He'd only tried to protect her. Apparently she didn't need protecting. Didn't she understand it was second nature to him as an officer of the law? Make that an ex-officer, ex-detective with the Portland Police Department.

He rolled away. "Stay down."

Zach crept over to hide behind the snowmobiles, trying to get a look at who had fired the shot. Olivia crawled over to him and another bullet pinged against the snowmobile closest to her. Another hit the tree behind him.

To let the assailant know Zach had come armed and prepared, he reached for the weapon in his shoulder holster, chambered a round and fired toward the shooter to hold him off. Even though he was no longer a detective, he still carried a weapon, his concealed weapon permit legal anywhere in the state of Oregon. This incident confirmed the necessity.

He hoped the rounds he fired would hold off the shooter while he and Olivia made a quick plan.

"I said to stay down." He turned to look at her, softening his expression. She didn't seem to notice he'd snapped at her, but under the circumstances, that hardly mattered.

She glared at him. "I'm not a child."

Take that back. She *had* noticed his harsh tone. "Someone is shooting at us. At you. What's going on, Olivia?"

"I don't know." She crouched behind her snowmobile, a few feet from him.

Entirely too far away for him to adequately shield her if needed.

"We can't stay here." He searched the woods around them to make sure they were not being ambushed from behind.

"But we're safe behind the snowmobiles for now, aren't we?" she asked.

"If there's more than one shooter, we're going to get pinned down if we sit here."

Zach listened for movement, but all he heard was the gentle sound of snow falling through the trees. Unfortunately, the soft white stuff created a cushioned ground and would likely mute the shooter's approach if he decided to move in.

"What do you suggest?" Olivia inched close enough for him to see the flecks of gold in her warm cinnamon eyes.

Zach used to vacation here with his best friend Rich—Olivia's brother—and his family. A lot had happened since the last time he'd been here. But he'd never forget that special summer fourteen years ago when he was seventeen and Olivia had turned fifteen—it had been the first time he'd thought of her as more than Rich's kid sister. Four years later he was on the cusp of entering the police academy and proposing marriage to Olivia when it all fell apart. *Not now! Not now...* Terror filled her eyes, yanking him back. Gripping his heart and squeezing. He shoved the memories away. "I'm thinking." He peered around the bow of the vehicle. Nothing. He saw nothing but wilderness.

"Well, think faster." Olivia slid away from him.

"I don't know the area like you do," he said. "So you're going to have to lead us out of here."

"You mean on foot?"

He nodded. "We're not getting out of here on the snowmobiles, at least not yet. We'd be too exposed if we got on them now. We can't risk it."

He eyed the area on this side of the vehicles. Through the white-frosted evergreens he spotted a slope.

Zach gestured toward it. "Where does that lead?"

"There's a dip down to a small brook."

"Where will it take us?"

Olivia shrugged. "Away from here."

A spray of bullets splintered the trees near them. A semiautomatic. Once again, Zach's protective nature reared up and he reached for Olivia, wrapping his arms and body around her like a shield to cover her.

The shooters—and now he was certain there was more than one who carried rapid-firing deadly weapons—weren't backing down.

If Rich had only given him more information he could have prepared.

He couldn't have imagined he'd be following a trail of blood and snowmobile tracks to find Olivia out here in the wilderness searching for her brother. And now as he looked at her, he saw the girl he'd once loved had grown into a beautiful, capable woman. Her reddish-brown locks spilled from beneath the helmet, curling around the collar of her black-and-pink snowmobile suit, and the eyes that stared at him now could hurt him all over again if he let her.

But that wasn't important.

What mattered most was that he had to keep her safe and track down her brother before the shooters killed them all. And find out *why* someone was shooting at them. Olivia and Rich's life depended on Zach now. The irony! He'd relinquished the job he loved and was no longer a police officer or a detective.

Maybe he was no longer officially sworn to protect, but the motto remained in his bones.

If only he hadn't failed to protect when it mattered most.

TWO

Olivia screamed as bark splintered from the trees next to them. Why was someone shooting at them?

Zach's solid form shielded her, protected her. As much as she didn't like his proximity, she couldn't think what else to do.

He grabbed her shoulders, his face near hers. "Stick close to me, we're getting out of here, but keep low. Once we slide down far enough that the hill can protect us, we have to run for it."

Dazed, she stared at him.

"Are you listening?" He shook her shoulders.

She nodded but still struggled to comprehend what was happening.

"Think, Olivia, where are we going to run to? Where can we hide? You have to take us there."

"Okay, I got it."

Would anyone hear all the rapid gunfire? If they did, she doubted they would think much about it. People often took to the woods to practice shooting.

God, please let someone come to investigate and help us!

She pressed herself deep into the snow like Zach had

done and slid down the slope. Except they left a big fat trail that anyone could follow.

Now she wished the snowfall would break completely through the canopy and cover their path. If they could make it to a clearing, or where the trees weren't so thick, maybe they could lose the shooters. But then they'd be easy targets. No good solution presented itself.

"Hurry," Zach whispered.

He'd already dropped to the brook. Olivia's pounding heart leaped to her throat.

Shoving, pushing hard, she slid until she was far enough down the hill that she could crouch without getting hit by a bullet. Then she hiked the rest of the way down to Zach.

Determination flashed in his gaze as he grabbed her gloved hand. Together they followed the nearly frozen brook, running where they could, and slowing in places where the snow grew too deep. With the effort, white clouds puffed out as her lungs labored to supply oxygen to her frantic heart.

Life and death.

This was a matter of life and death.

Hadn't she wanted a quiet life? She'd moved here from Portland to put distance between her and tragedy. And now…this. Anger churned inside, fueling her strides.

Rich had done this. There was no other explanation. Olivia had asked why he'd come back to the States and he'd replied that he was finished working for the private military contract security company in the Middle East. He'd been restless, if not distressed.

Oh, Rich. What have you gotten yourself into? What have you gotten us into?

He'd brought these men here after him. She knew

that in her gut. And now they were after her, too. Her and Zach. The man she wanted to forget, along with all that had gone wrong in her life, was in the mix, as well. Though he'd taken the lead, she pushed ahead of him. He didn't know where to go. He didn't know the area like she did and had said as much.

Still, she needed to hear from him. Did he have any ideas? An escape plan? "Where do you want me to take us, Zach? Where should we head?"

"Let's lead them away from the snowmobiles, lose them, and then we can backtrack so we can ride out of here."

She ducked under a branch. A bullet sliced across her helmet.

"Olivia!" Zach pushed her to the ground again.

"Will you stop doing that?" She pushed him off.

"Get behind the trees!"

She did as he asked, and together they crawled over and hid behind a thick-trunked pine—wide enough they could both press their backs against it. Catching her breath, she looked up and watched huge flakes dance on the air and flutter down toward her. They landed on her face and stuck in her lashes. She blinked them away.

Pulling her helmet off, she examined the damage. That had been close, much too close. She stashed it to the side, intending to leave it behind. The bright pink of the helmet had been intentional, meant to be visible in the woods to prevent hunters from shooting her by mistake. But now wasn't the time for visibility.

"Good idea." Zach peered at her, nodding his approval. "If anything, that helmet makes you an easy target."

His icy blues turned more intense. Olivia peered out into the woods, looking anywhere and at anything except Zach. Sitting this close to him when she'd wanted to forget him, and having him with her in this far too surreal situation, would be her undoing if the shooters didn't get her first.

"But without the helmet, you're far too exposed." He tugged his white helmet off. "Take mine."

She whipped her gaze around to his. Yeah. Much too close. "What? No. Zach," she whispered. "I'm not wearing your helmet. So put that back on."

"I didn't ask."

Fury boiled inside. "I don't need your protection."

Hurt flickered in his gaze then vanished behind a stone cold stare. *Oh... I didn't mean to say that.* She hadn't meant to hurt him. When would it ever end?

Her legs trembled with fear and her lips weren't far behind. She wouldn't let him see her like this—a weak, scared little girl—though why she wanted to hide that from him she wasn't sure. After all, someone was trying to kill them and she *was* scared. There wasn't any reason to be ashamed of that. But she didn't want him to protect her. She didn't want to be that vulnerable.

Did she have a choice?

And wasn't Zach scared, too? Trying to read his mind, sense his emotional state, wouldn't do either of them any good. Again, she averted her gaze, listening, watching for the shooters as she caught her breath.

Zach gently touched her chin and turned her to face him. "Are you okay?"

It hurt when he touched her like that, all gentle and caring. She didn't want that from him, or for him to see that she was absolutely not okay. But he probably already knew. "I don't know how to answer that."

He studied her, his blue-eyed gaze seeming to soak

up every inch of her face. For a split second, she worried about her appearance. But she'd long ago given up the smoky eye shadow, snow plum blush and deep mauve lipstick she used to put on for him. Her self-consciousness fell away as she realized he hadn't donned the helmet after her refusal to wear it, and that gave her ample opportunity to take him in up close and personal. That smattering of day-old stubble across his strong jaw. A few crow's-feet that hadn't yet emerged around his intense blue eyes when she'd last been this close to him. Protection practically spilled off him. That and something she couldn't read behind his gaze. But maybe she shouldn't even try.

Still…what was he thinking?

"We need to get moving." He hesitated, then asked, "Can you lead us the long way around to the snowmobiles so we can get out of here? That is, if they haven't already disabled the machines so we couldn't do just that."

"I can try. But what about Rich? I still need to find him. I can't leave without him."

She hadn't wanted to entertain the possibility that Rich was already dead. She wouldn't let her thoughts go there, but the hope she'd held on to was quickly slipping away.

"We'll find him, don't worry. But don't forget he's ex-military. He's trained to survive. My priority is getting you to safety." Zach suddenly stiffened and angled his head. He ducked low and peered around the tree. "Time to go."

Zach stood and clambered around as he pressed his back against the tree. "I'm going to hold them off. You keep hidden behind the trees as you run and try get as far away as you can. Just keep going."

"What? I thought you wanted us to make our way back

to the snowmobiles? I'm not leaving you. I don't want to find Rich only to have to come back and find you."

"You won't have to find me. I'll be right behind you. I'm just giving you a head start."

Zach aimed and fired off his weapon, the sound ricocheting through her head, ringing in her ears. Okay, well, maybe she could put some distance between them.

He fired another round, and then another in rapid succession. She wished for her own weapon, the one she'd left at home. She could help Zach. He would run out of ammo soon.

"Go, Olivia. I'll find you. I can't hold them off forever. Don't make me waste these bullets."

Just as she would have turned from him, he grabbed her collar and pulled her face close to his. His chest rose and fell, and the intensity in his eyes as he appeared to drink her in stole her breath away. "Be careful out there, Olivia. Don't take any chances. I promise I'll find you."

For a split second, in the midst of lethal danger, her mind flooded with memories of kissing him. Her senses tingled. Her breaths came quicker, but not from the danger. Then he pushed away. "Go!"

She scrambled from him, keeping to the trees as he fired. She had to make this count and try to hide as she escaped.

Deep inside she felt like she was running from much more than bullets. She was running from past hurts she'd wanted to forget—she was running from Zachary Long.

Was there any way out of this situation, any possibility of survival that didn't include Zach doing the thing he loved, the thing he'd left her for—serving and protecting? Risking his life for her. She should be glad she had a police officer, a detective, here to help her through this. But she couldn't bring herself to be glad for it.

He loved the danger. The thrill of it ran through his blood since he came from a family of police officers, but Olivia had lost too much already with the death of her own police officer father when she was just eighteen. And she wasn't willing to go through that again.

A bullet whizzed too closely and hit a tree to her right. She ducked, then crouched as she moved between a copse of Douglas firs and ponderosa pines. Would Zach be able to hold them off? And even if he did, then what?

What about him? How was he going to survive and find her? And just where should she go? Questions barraged her when she wanted tunnel vision, to focus on a single goal.

Running for her life. Escaping.

She pressed on, plowing through waist-deep snow, gripping branches for support in her push to escape, to get far from the assailants. All the while, she never stopped searching the woods for any sign of Rich.

There was none.

It was as if he'd simply disappeared from that snowmobile.

She believed he hadn't fallen into the hands of these guys after them or else why were they after her and Zach if they had the person they'd come for? Could she be wrong about all of it?

Finally, exhaustion slowed her efforts. Her sluggish legs burning, Olivia leaned against a tree. She would wait for Zach here while she caught her breath. Rest her muscles, slow the hammer in her heart.

He would never find her if she didn't stop. As her breathing calmed, she had the chance to get her bearings.

A few feet from where she stood the ground dropped away into a deep fissure—a crack at least seventy feet deep or more. She knew about it from her summer hikes, but in the winter hidden dangers grew more treacherous. Snow and ice covered the fissure, hiding it in places.

She would definitely need to wait here for Zach, if for no other reason than to warn him and keep him from plummeting to his death in the crevice. She wasn't sure if it was wrong but she wished that fate on the shooters.

A brutal storm moved in quickly. Could her predicament get any worse? Still, a raging snowstorm, possibly with blizzard-force winds, would also be a problem for the bad guys. They'd need shelter, too, and they couldn't follow Zach and Olivia's footprints.

A new cause for panic settled in her chest. Zach hadn't caught up with her yet. In a snowstorm, would he be able to find her? Here she was hoping the storm would hide her tracks from the shooters, but if Zach hadn't found her by then, he never would.

A twig snapped. Someone approached—had they seen her? Once again she found herself asking if she would see friend or foe. She'd long ago lost her knife in the scramble down to the brook. She grabbed a big branch she could use for a weapon and waited, the element of surprise her only advantage.

A figured moved past. She recognized Zach's thick head of wheat hair as he stumbled forward into the deep snow around the group of Douglas firs where she'd been hiding. He'd followed her tracks, just as they would. But she was more than glad to see him.

"Zach!"

Bending next to him, she grabbed his arm and assisted him up and out of the thick white powder. Then Olivia threw her arms around him. "Zach, I was afraid you wouldn't find me before the snow covered my tracks."

She quickly dropped her arms and looked him up and down. "Are you hurt?"

He shook his head, too out of breath to answer her. Then finally, "They're not too far behind so we need to keep moving. If we're fortunate, we'll get a blizzard."

Zach had been counting on her to lead the way since she'd had many summers to explore the area before she'd made the vacation home permanent. With Rich's sudden appearance, and just as sudden disappearance, and then the shooters, she'd been slow to process the events.

But beyond this stand of firs, she remembered the orange-trunked madrone trees and a few maples before the rocks. And then…

"Come on, I know where we can hide."

He angled his head, his intense gaze catching hers, radiating reassurance as if to say, *I knew you would.*

His confidence in her had her heart dancing when it shouldn't, especially in the middle of this threat. Still, she could use that to bolster her courage.

"Come on." She held out her hand and he took it.

Olivia pointed out the fissure to Zach, just to be sure he wouldn't fall to his death if he came back this way.

"I think I remember that from before."

"Good. Just making sure. But you know what, maybe we could lure the shooters this way, trick them into falling in."

Zach's face twisted up. "Only as a last resort. No. Just no."

"Fine."

And as Zach had wished, the wind drove the snow hard into icy pinpricks against her face. They might even find themselves in a whiteout. Bad news, but they could use this development to their advantage.

Olivia kept to the trees as she led Zach, holding his hand as they hiked through what seemed like bottomless layers of snow in places, and up a rocky incline. She slipped once on iced-over rocks, but Zach's hands slid around her waist and assisted her up and forward. Even without the heavy, driving snow to cover their trail, they could have already lost their pursuers in this treacherous part of the wilderness.

Zach hadn't asked her exactly where she led them, which meant he trusted her to find the way. The longer it took, the more she began to doubt her sense of direction. She'd been here many times as a kid, but hadn't come back even once since living at the cabin. Maybe all the gunfire and fear had confused her sense of direction.

But she kept moving, plowing and hiking forward. Now they faced off with a rocky wall, snow and ice catching in between the small cracks and fissures.

The cave had to be here somewhere.

And then it hit her. Would Rich have come here, too, knowing it was here? Had he thought to hide in the cave just like Olivia had?

Her hopes jumped.

She glanced back at Zach. He'd left his helmet behind, but he'd long ago covered his head with the hood on his winter coat, as had Olivia, so she couldn't see his eyes at that moment. Maybe that was a good thing. She returned her energy to finding the cave, pressing her hands against the rocks as she went. Even though she wore gloves, her fingers grew stiff and clumsy.

One look at Zach's red cheeks and she knew the truth. The dropping temperature was getting to them.

And what of their pursuers? Did the shooters realize they could die if they didn't find shelter, too? If the men after Rich were anything like him, then they too were survivors and were prepared for anything, carrying their bivouac gear with them in the mountains on their murderous hunting trip. Olivia's shred of hope took a dive.

But why should she focus on them? She had yet to find the cave that would keep her and Zach warm, two people who hadn't carried bivouac gear with them.

God, please, where is the cave? We have to find the cave!

Worry and doubt threaded through her thoughts. Did she have the wrong place, after all? And if she did, how would they survive?

If that was the case, they were as good as dead.

No. Olivia wouldn't accept that. She cleared away the morbid thoughts and kept her gloved hands pressed against the rock wall, letting it guide her inward until she found the small opening.

There.

"It's here," she croaked out, almost not recognizing her own voice. Relief swirled through her.

The rock walls extending forward and out on both sides of the slender gap that served as the cave entrance saved them from the brunt of the building storm.

She hesitated before rushing in and turned to Zach. "If Rich could have made it here, this is where he would be hiding."

Olivia dreaded looking in Zach's eyes. What would she see in them? She wanted to cling to the smallest of hopes, but he could shatter those with one look.

He was a realist, after all.

"Let me go first." Zach lifted his gun, gripped her

hand and pulled her along behind him. "The shooters. They could have found the cave ahead of us. They might be waiting inside."

"Stay here, just at the entrance." Zach released her hand.

Olivia sucked in a breath as if she would counter him but then, surprising him, she nodded in agreement. The storm forced them to seek shelter and this cave served as their best option. But would he lead them inside to their deaths?

Or had Rich taken shelter here like she'd suggested?

"If the worst happens, you turn and run." He pressed forward without waiting for her answer.

Sworn to protect.

Like that had worked so well.

He ignored his doubts and shoved his fears aside.

Entering the dark opening, he crept forward, weapon poised to fire, until his eyes adjusted to the darkness. If the shooters had taken shelter in the cave or waited for Olivia and Zach there, they could take Zach out before he was the wiser. He listened for movement, for breathing, anything at all, as he hedged the rock wall. The shooters weren't the only possible threat. They could walk in on a hibernating bear.

Memories of this cave skittered through him. Rich had brought him here a few times in the summer. But that had been years ago and Zach wouldn't count on his memory to guide him.

"Anyone here?" he asked.

Not that he expected someone with nefarious intentions to respond, but maybe Rich had come to hide here like Olivia hoped.

Zach had heard that hope in her words, and a sliver of pain skated over his heart. He had a feeling she would be disappointed.

She rushed by him, stumbling forward in the dark. “Rich! Are you in here?”

“What are you doing?” He grabbed her arm and pulled her back against him. “I told you to wait. Maybe the bad guys aren’t in here, but we could disturb a bear.”

“Rich!” Tears edged her voice.

But nobody answered.

She shifted forward and Zach caught her up in his arms to steady her. “I’m sorry, Olivia. So sorry.”

He never could have imagined he’d find her in his arms again. Good thing her bulky snowmobile suit served as a protective barrier. He didn’t want to feel her softness or be reminded of his attraction to her that obviously had remained even after a decade.

Zach would help her and support her now because she needed it, but he’d guard his heart against falling for her again—an act that would require all his strength. With his hands somehow in the silky copper locks that fell around her shoulders, and her distraught form leaning against him, Zach admitted that he could easily slip back into the past with her.

Except he couldn’t forget how she’d hurt him, asking him to give up his dream for her, then breaking it all off when he didn’t. He would use that now to stay free of any entanglement and continue to forge a future without her, though he found himself holding her in his arms once again.

Seeming to read his mind, she stiffened and moved away, swiping at her face. “I’m sorry, I didn’t mean to—”

“Don’t worry about it.” He cut her off and moved deeper into the cave, holding his weapon tightly in his grip. Though if anyone waited here, they would already have made their presence known.

Zach and Olivia could have been killed in that one moment of indiscretion.

"The cave doesn't go back very far," she said. "Maybe a few yards. I doubt there's a bear in here or we would know it by now. Bad guys, too. Besides, I can't believe they could find this cave. Even in the summer it's well hidden. Forget about it in the winter, especially with the approaching storm."

"We don't know if they scouted the area before their attack. We can't be too careful."

Zach's eyes adjusted to the dim light spilling through the cave's opening along with the cold and snow. The weather looked bleak out there and made him grateful they'd found this temporary shelter.

"Might as well get comfortable." Olivia put her hand against the wall and slid down to the hard ground, her boots scraping dirt and pebbles. She wrapped her arms around herself.

The cave's temperature was much warmer than outside, but even wearing the snowmobile garb, he could feel the cold seeping in. Zach frowned. They had nothing with which to make a fire. He wasn't sure they'd want to risk giving themselves away even if they could build one.

Remaining standing, he watched the entrance in case any moment one of the men who had been shooting at them entered the cave to shelter from the storm, too. He and Olivia could have been followed.

He glanced down at her. She'd leaned her head against her knees, hair spilling over her back and shoulders. He wanted to dispel the memories and the sudden longing to hold her, but just as he would have looked away, she lifted her head, her cinnamon eyes capturing his gaze.

"I was shocked to see you today, Zach. The men shooting at us, that whole thing was a shocker, too. But you appeared out of nowhere."

Yeah, he got that. He hadn't been expecting to see her either. It was here in the Siskiyous that he'd first fallen in love with her one summer. But seeing her in the flesh today? His throat grew tight.

"Seeing you surprised me, too, but when you think about it, it makes sense," he said.

"Right. You were Rich's best friend, maybe you still are. But obviously you came here to meet him for some reason. He didn't know I was living here and acted downright put out to see me."

Zach shifted then leaned against the rock wall. He'd watch the entrance another hour. If the men didn't find the cave within that time, he doubted they would. Besides, they likely had their own supplies to set up a shelter or found an empty cabin somewhere. An empty house like the Kendricks'.

If not, they'd die in this weather.

"How did he seem?"

Olivia stretched her legs and leaned against the wall behind her, resting her head. "Something was wrong. I knew that I should have paid more attention. But I was so glad to see him and thought maybe whatever was disturbing him had to do with the job he left. So I dreamed that he could stay here and work with me at Wilderness, Inc. for a while. Coop even said he could use a new guide. I was on my way back from Gideon and talking to Coop about using Rich as a guide. He knows the area. And business has been good."

"Coop?"

"Cooper Wilde. He runs Wilderness, Inc. here in the mountains out of Gideon. It's an adventure excursion and wilderness training business. Anyway, I guess this answers the question about what happened to Rich."

"What do you mean?"

"I followed the snowmobile tracks from the house. There was blood, Zach. Blood on the snow. It had to be Rich's. The guys shooting at us? All I can think is they were after him and he took a bullet, maybe, before he ran and got away on his snowmobile."

"We can't know for sure, but that sounds like one possibility. Regardless, it seems they want to kill us, whatever the reason."

If those men were after Rich and he had led them here, to his sister… Zach paced the cave, fisting his gloved hand and squeezing the pistol grip with his other. Every choice a person made could have catastrophic effects on everyone else. He'd experienced that firsthand and felt the repercussions of his own decisions to the marrow in his bones.

"If only we could find Rich," Olivia said. "Make sure he's safe, help him if he's hurt. I'm worried about him out there in this storm, maybe even bleeding to death."

"Nothing we can do about it."

Olivia shot him a glare. He knew she saw the change in him—that he'd hardened over the years. Inwardly, he sighed, wishing for the younger version of himself.

He didn't like the thought of Rich suffering out there either and should be more reassuring to his friend's sister. "If I know anything about your brother, it's that he has survival skills, and he's out there surviving, making it through this storm, just like us. We have to trust that Rich will rely on his training."

If he isn't already dead.

THREE

Olivia had seen Rich's pack on the bed. He hadn't taken time to gather supplies before he fled for his life. She couldn't share Zach's confidence in her brother's training.

She studied Zach as he watched the cave entrance. Her heart skipped a little. Back in high school, he'd been the kind of guy every girl could fall for, and now, to her chagrin, he looked even better.

He exhibited a kind of masculinity that was hard to resist. Skilled and confident. But those skills were the very thing that stood between them and had torn them apart. That and the choices he'd made.

Olivia shoved thoughts of the past away and focused on the very real and dangerous present. What else did Zach know about her brother? Why had Rich asked him to meet at the house? Her teeth chattered, preventing her from voicing the questions.

Shivering, she tucked her knees up against her chest and rested her chin on them again. How were they going to make it through tonight without a fire, even in this cave? It wasn't deep enough to prevent the snow from swirling in, ushered by the ice-cold wind that had ramped up.

She buried her face in her knees, trying to keep the cold at bay.

Zach clomped across the cave and stood next to her. He slid down the wall and scooted right up close to her.

"What…what are you doing?" she asked.

"You're cold. I'm cold."

She thought to shift away from him but his body heat drew her, though reluctantly. Then he wrapped his arm around her, pulling her closer to him, nice and tight. "Come on, Olivia. We have to keep warm. The past is the past, and we can keep it there. No need to dredge up what happened before. At the moment we're just two people doing what we have to do in order to survive, right?"

She nodded. "Well, when you put it that way."

When she peeked at him, he showed her that half grin she remembered and liked. What was he thinking? She wasn't sure she wanted to know, but she accepted the warmth he offered then pressed her face into her knees again. Maybe she'd warm up enough after a while to scoot away from him. But right now, she couldn't think straight. Somehow she had to come to grips with everything that had happened over the last several hours. Images swirled like snowflakes in her mind.

Rich's disappearance.

The blood in the snow.

The snowmobile tracks.

The men with the guns.

And…Zach.

She could hardly believe she was waiting out a storm in this cave with him and that he had his strong arm around her. Life had a way of going in circles. He was right—without survival gear, they had no choice but to use their body heat to stay warm. They couldn't risk discovery by building a fire when lunatics pursued them, openly firing at them, shooting to kill. She hated that these men had turned the woods she loved into a crime scene.

And Rich. *God, please, please keep him safe wherever he is out there.*

"So, what's the plan then?" she asked.

"It's pretty simple. Stay warm and alive until the storm passes. We might even be here all night. Then in the morning we find our way back to civilization and keep well away from those shooters. Maybe we can find Rich, too."

"Tell me about Rich. Until he showed up yesterday, I hadn't talked to him in a long time."

"I haven't spoken to him that much myself. I'm sure you at least know he's been in the Middle East working security for a private military contractor."

"That was the last thing I knew about." Grief thickened in her throat. So much of what she felt inside couldn't be spoken out loud because it involved Zach's own personal tragedy.

And the mistake he'd made that had cost his sister's life. Olivia wouldn't add to his torment by bringing it up. He seemed to sense she needed a moment to process. His thoughts had likely turned to the past, as well.

But in this moment, regret permeated her bones.

Why hadn't she talked to Rich? Why had she been so quick to blame him for their mother's death? Four years ago, he'd been grieving the death of his fiancée—Zach's sister, Sarah—and after his tour of duty was over, he decided he wouldn't return to the States, after all, because there would be no bride waiting for him.

No wedding.

So he took that job in private security instead.

Their mother had taken his absence too hard, just like she had Dad's death when he'd been killed in the line of duty with the Portland PD. Her mother had used alcohol to console herself for a couple of years after their father's death but had found her way to sobriety and had been sober until Sarah had been killed and Rich made the decision to stay away. Mom had needed him, perhaps too much. Their mother had been killed in a drunk-driving accident when her vehicle ran off a bridge.

Olivia had blamed Rich and hadn't spoken to him since Mom's funeral three years ago.

She squeezed her eyes against the tears threatening to spill. He had needed time and space to heal. Olivia could hardly blame him for that. It was exactly the reason she'd resigned her job as a biology teacher in Portland two years ago and moved to the family vacation house situated in the pristine wilderness of the Siskiyou Mountains. She'd wanted a new life and had run from all that had gone wrong in her old one. And until yesterday, when Rich had shown up, peace and solace had filled her days, replacing tragedy and drama.

But her efforts had been for nothing. Trouble had found her out in the middle of nowhere.

Now she realized she had wasted those precious years avoiding communication with her brother. Her mission now was to find him and keep him in her life. Somehow. Someway.

She buried the pain of the past encroaching on her present situation—and entered survival mode. Clearing tears from her throat, she asked, "What else can you tell me?"

"Not much, I'm sorry. He called me three days ago

and asked me to meet him today. Said it was urgent but he couldn't tell me anything more. In fact, he didn't mention the cabin by name, only the place we used to vacation together. Until I got there, I wasn't completely sure he'd meant your family's cabin. It wasn't the only place we went in the summer. He said he couldn't trust anyone except me. Obviously, he was in some kind of trouble."

The wind whipped flakes around, driving them deep into the cave to blanket them as they huddled together. Zach brushed the snow off them both.

"Do you think it has something to do with his job?" she asked. "He told me he was done working for them."

"We can't know when he was done or how long he's even been back in the States."

"I thought you guys were best friends."

Right, and she was his sister. She felt his gaze on her, but stared straight ahead and puzzled over the rough drawings that she and Rich had carved in the wall as children. They had somehow remained after all this time.

"Life happens. People go their separate ways. He had a job on the other side of the world, and I had mine here. I think Sarah's death changed him. Talking to me, well, that just reminded him of what he'd lost and my part in it." Zach's voice had turned harsh.

Yeah, she got that. Though Olivia had not been super close to Sarah, the woman had been her brother's fiancée, and of course, the sister of the guy she used to love. Sarah's death had changed their lives in ways they couldn't have imagined. Olivia tried not to think about the burden that put on Zach, who blamed himself for her death.

Still, she didn't like the harsh, cold tone coming from him. That wasn't the Zach she'd known, but she had to get over it. Like he'd said, they were just two people doing what they had to in order to survive.

They weren't a couple again. They weren't in love. How he sounded shouldn't matter to her. Besides, he'd hurt her, choosing danger over love. Choosing to become a police officer like his father instead of being with Olivia.

After losing her father, who'd been shot and killed during a simple traffic stop, Olivia knew she couldn't handle that life. Couldn't handle being married to a police officer. She thought Zach had understood that, and yet he'd still chosen that path. His dream had been more important to him than her.

Regardless, Sarah's death had affected them in ways they couldn't have imagined.

All their lives had been wrapped up in a big tangled mess of tragedy from which each of them had tried to escape, and yet here they were, tangled up together again.

She drew in a shuddering breath.

Zach squeezed her. "Hey, are you okay?"

No! No, she wasn't okay. But talking about it would just dredge it all up again and hadn't he said they didn't want to do that? How could Zach not be thinking about everything that had happened? She leaned forward and pushed his arm off her. She'd leaned against him for the warmth. That made sense, but she didn't need his arm around her for that.

Not now.

Not ever.

She wasn't the least surprised when the storm's intensity increased and the wind picked up, creating an eerie howl in the cave to add to her torment.

* * *

Zach sensed the subtle shift in her attitude, the change in her. He'd hoped they could endure and survive their predicament without the past coming between them, but clearly, ignoring their familiar surroundings and forgetting the memories had been hoping for too much.

"Try to get some sleep, if you can," he offered.

He might find the situation as intolerable as she obviously did if he let his mind drift back.

Instead, he would think about her brother, Rich. Zach hadn't wanted Olivia to know just how concerned he had been for his friend. But things didn't look good. Sure, he believed the guy's survival training could keep him alive until help reached him, but these circumstances didn't bode well for Rich. In fact, Zach feared that even he and Olivia wouldn't escape unscathed, though he would do his best to get her somewhere safe.

But with his track record, he didn't know if his efforts would be enough.

What kind of trouble forced Rich to flee to the family cabin? Brought men to this neck of the Siskiyou Mountains in order to kill him? And yeah, Zach concurred with Olivia's assessment that the men who'd shot at Zach and Olivia had been after Rich, too, but Zach hadn't said that out loud.

As a former detective, he didn't want to jump to conclusions, even when they appeared obvious. He couldn't begin to presume what kind of trouble Rich had brought with him to Olivia's door. To be fair, Rich hadn't known he would find his sister here, any more than Zach had.

That didn't prevent Zach's rising fury with Rich for involving Olivia, even though Zach had brought trouble to his own sister.

Trouble that had cost her life.

He couldn't stand by and watch the same happen to Olivia.

As if sensing his tumultuous thoughts, she shifted against him, trying to get comfortable, then finally turned her back to him and leaned against his shoulder. His insides ached with her nearness.

Sweet Olivia. How did he keep her safe?

God, I need Your help.

That's what Rich would want from him now—to protect his sister. They weren't going anywhere in this storm, especially with nightfall fast approaching. The only thing left to do involved wrapping his arms around her as they sat in the cave and tried to stay warm without a fire. But Olivia wouldn't have that, and frankly, he didn't want it either. He'd said they should leave the past behind them.

Right. He still felt the sting of her rejection as if it had happened yesterday.

What was the matter with him?

Memories, that's what. This close to the woman he used to love and his mind flashed right back as if ten years had never passed. Except…well, the pain of his hurt surged all over again.

He'd had to follow his calling. His lot in life. He'd had to become a police officer and work his way up to detective like his father and grandfather before him. That was in his blood. Olivia knew that. He couldn't understand why she would give him up because he had to follow his dream. Her father had been an officer, as well, God rest his soul. She hadn't loved Zach enough to let him be who he was supposed to be.

In an ironic twist, he'd given it all up anyway a year ago. The cost of following his dream had been too high.

First, his decision to join the police force had cost him Olivia, and then his subsequent failure had been like a domino effect. Had he succeeded in protecting his sister, Sarah, she would still be alive and Rich would be married to her. Maybe Olivia and Rich's mother would still be alive.

He groaned, hating where this night in the cave with the wind howling like an underscore to his past tragedies drove him. Closing his eyes, he tried to clear his mind. When he opened them again, he couldn't see his hand in front of his face.

"Zach?" Olivia whispered next to him. "Are you awake?"

"Yeah."

"It's dark in here."

And cold.

She hadn't said the words but he figured she didn't want to admit she needed anything like, say, warmth.

"You're not scared of the dark, are you?" Zach grinned to himself. In the dark. Olivia would never *admit* she was scared either.

"Of course not. It's just unnerving. I thought I heard something scurrying around in here. You don't think there's a rodent or a raccoon or any number of other possible creatures sharing the cave with us, do you?"

"It's hard to say but I don't have a flashlight or a match, so we'll just have to tough it out." And, since he remained cold as well, and knew she would never admit she needed his warmth again, he wrapped his arm around her and drew her in close.

She didn't resist.

There. That would keep them both warmer. Now only one thing remained. Waiting. They would wait for the storm to go and wait for morning to come. Seemed like there was a Bible verse on that theme that he'd learned somewhere in Sunday school class. The thought caught him by surprise.

Zachary hadn't prayed in far too long. Maybe he'd been mad at God for everything he'd lost, but he tried not to think about it. Just ignored that aspect of his life, but now, here alone in the blackest darkness he'd ever experienced, just him and Olivia in this cave where the wind would probably howl all night, sitting close to one of his biggest hurts, biggest regrets, he thought maybe God was trying to get his attention.

"It's going to be all right, Olivia. We're going to make it through." He wasn't sure why he felt the need to say the words, but maybe it had a whole lot to do with wanting to sound off something positive to combat the doleful cry of the wind in the cave.

She scooted closer to him and shivered. He held her tight until her breathing shifted to a steady slow rhythm that told him she'd finally fallen asleep. Then he let himself drift, too. He didn't know what they would face tomorrow and he didn't want to borrow trouble, but he needed to rest. Needed his strength.

Except the worst of dreams accosted his restless sleep.

"Detective Long. You recognize my voice?"

"Jimmy Delaney." The man had gotten out of prison a week ago. What did he want? Why was he calling?

Fear clawed through Zach.

"That's right. I have someone here with me you might miss."

"Zach?" Sarah's voice rasped, then she sobbed. "Zach..." A scream broke through.

"What do you want?" Zach let all the anger he pos-

sessed pour through the phone connection. He would kill Jimmy Delaney when he got his hands on him.

"You. Just you."

Then gunfire split his eardrums.

A sound stirred Zach awake and he bolted to his feet, rousing Olivia, too. "What was that?"

"What?" She glanced up, sleep clinging to her eyes.

"I heard something."

He grabbed his weapon, his palm still slick from the recurring nightmare that always hit him at his lowest. Of course he would relive that day, that bad dream, here in this cave under these circumstances.

He shook it away and waited, listening and watching the entrance.

The storm had stopped. Morning light spilled through the opening.

Had it brought the men who wanted to kill them?

A rifle shot rang out somewhere in the woods near them, echoing through the cave.

FOUR

Gunfire jolted Olivia fully awake. She attempted to stand, but her body, stiff from sitting on the hard ground in a cold cave all night, refused to cooperate. Zach assisted her to her feet before she could protest.

"Thank you." She rubbed her arms to get the blood going and noted his attention on the more urgent matters outside the cave entrance. Had they been discovered?

She'd much prefer coffee to the fear curdling in her stomach. "What are we going to do?"

Zach edged to the cave opening, staying in the shadows created by the rays of light spilling in. So focused on his task, Olivia wasn't sure he'd even heard her question.

Then, finally, "First I'm going to check around outside and see if it's safe."

"And?"

"Then we're getting out of here."

"And what if it's not safe? What if those men are out there? And what about Rich? We have to find him, or at least, if you're not willing, then I have to find him." Oh, why had she said that? But she needed to make him understand.

He turned to look at her then. Under the cold intensity of his ice-blue eyes, she was hard pressed not to look away, but she held his gaze.

"One thing at a time," he said. "Besides, I don't think the gunfire we heard was meant for us. That was a rifle. Not a semiautomatic like the shooters used. Like mine."

Olivia closed the distance then. Approaching Zach, she stood just behind him and peered outside into the winter wonderland. Standing this close, she could once again feel the heat emanating from him. Olivia felt chilled to the bone and wished she could have his arms around her again. Finding the thought surprisingly much too comfortable, she took a step back. She couldn't let herself grow attached to him again. He'd just leave her to return to his job with the Portland PD.

She focused her thoughts on their predicament. Then whom had it been meant for? Rich? Her heart pounded too hard for this early in the morning, but she was worried for her brother. She hadn't gotten him back only to lose him again. And once they found him—and they would find him, she wouldn't think otherwise—she would never again let time and distance separate them. She'd keep in touch.

Pain burned behind her eyes. She had to stop thinking about Rich.

The gunfire hadn't been about him. Could it have been hunters? Olivia thought of the poachers she'd seen in the region killing deer out of season, and how furious she'd been. She'd reported them to the local game warden, but they had never been caught.

Zach tensed and stepped from the shadows and into the light, his form now silhouetted in the cave entrance.

"Stay here." He didn't bother glancing back to see if

she agreed, but stepped from the cave, expecting her to follow orders. Simple as that.

She ground her molars.

Then exhaled.

Her reaction to his instructions hadn't been fair to him. He'd only been trying to protect her. It was in his blood. Olivia should appreciate his protective nature. She should give him a break and be grateful, as well.

Crossing her arms, she waited.

And waited.

After twenty minutes, Olivia wasn't waiting anymore.

She crept from the cave, the gray light blinding her for a moment as she hugged the wall. She knew her way around, but wasn't certain about Zach. Inching along the rock wall that led out of the hidden entrance, Olivia pushed back her concern that something had happened to him. He was skilled and trained to handle criminals. He knew what he was doing.

Finally, she came to the place where she'd have to climb down over the snow-covered boulders. But she spotted Zach's path cutting into the thick white layers and followed his trail down as gusts of wind tossed snow around her. She tugged the hood of her jacket tight around her face.

Come on, Zach. Where are you?

She hadn't realized his searching the area meant disappearing for this long. At the bottom of the boulders, she hopped to the ground and sank to her waist. Great. She followed his more than obvious plow through the depths of white and then she spotted him. Hidden behind a thick fallen tree trunk that was almost unrecognizable after the storm, he peered out into the quiet forest, cold gusts making the white-frosted trees clack together and drop loads of snow.

She crept in close and, just as she reached forward to touch him, he whirled on her with his weapon aimed point-blank.

Olivia lifted her hands in surrender. "It's me."

Dropping his shoulders, he released an exaggerated breath and lowered his weapon. Eyes blazing, his gaze turned on her. "What were you thinking? I told you to stay in the cave."

Olivia moved next to him behind the trunk. "I'm not much for following orders."

He didn't answer for the longest time, so she risked a glance and caught him studying her. When she looked at him, that half grin cracked his face. And her heart skipped a little. Oh, no, not that. Please not that. How could his smile do that to her after a decade? She'd once thought her reaction to him had been the fluttering of a young woman's heart, but apparently her age and experience had nothing at all to do with it.

"Why are you looking at me like that?" she asked.

He dropped the grin and turned serious. "No reason that matters." Zach nodded, gesturing toward the woods. "There are a couple of guys out there."

"You think it's the shooters?"

"Could be. Or maybe it's someone else. I was waiting and watching, trying to decide."

She dragged in a breath. "Poachers, maybe it's my poachers."

"*Your* poachers?"

"Just a couple of men I've seen hunting the last two winters during the off-season. There was a sweet doe I'd see hanging around the woods near the house. She got to where she wasn't even afraid of me. I think the men killed her. I'd seen them out there in the area one day, and the next day she never came back. Makes me so mad. I've been hoping to take them down."

"I'm sorry about your doe."

"She wasn't my pet. That's not legal for one thing. And the other thing, it wouldn't have been best for her." Olivia thought of the doe's soft brown eyes when she'd lift her head and catch Olivia outside. The doe would stare at her for a few moments then go back to foraging. Olivia hoped it wasn't the doe's lack of fear of humans that had gotten her killed. "It was like…we had an understanding."

The half grin again, this time revealing his dimple. "I have no doubt that you'll succeed in getting your poachers. Surprised you haven't already."

She wasn't sure how to take that. Had he meant it as a compliment or was there a hidden meaning behind his words? "Thanks for the vote of confidence…I think."

"I meant that as a compliment, Olivia. You were always the nurturing type. Glad to see that hasn't changed."

Now, don't go complimenting me, please. I don't want to like you, at least not in the same way I once did.

Then she saw the men between the trees, heading in the opposite direction—one of them carrying a smallish deer—a doe?—over his shoulders. Now she understood what that gunfire had been about. They had illegally killed a deer. The two men wore the same hunter's garb she'd seen them in before. One wore a bright orange beanie, and the other a camo face mask. "It's my poachers!"

And this time, she had Zach with her. He was an officer of the law. He could do something. The hardest part about stopping them was catching them in the act. That was what the game warden had said. In the act or holding the illegally killed animal for evidence.

"Hey!" She ran out from behind the boulder after them. "Hey, you!"

This was a bad idea. Probably why she hadn't bothered to ask Zach his opinion. She knew what he would've said. And now he had to expose himself to run after Olivia. She'd given them both away. "Come back!"

But it was too late. Still, poachers weren't usually murderers, too. They'd get slapped with a fine, if that. Poaching wasn't a capital crime.

She expected him to confront the hunters, but she didn't know he was no longer a police officer, wasn't carrying a badge, though even if he were, he'd be operating outside of his jurisdiction. Still, in Oregon the law would simply require him to obtain authorization, when practical, after the fact.

That is, if he were still a law enforcement officer.

Olivia wanted him to use the force of the law behind his badge and arrest these men carrying hunting rifles and an illegal kill. She'd always been passionate about animals, about wildlife. And with her sad story of the doe she loved, poachers beware.

Reluctantly, he trailed after her. With what they had faced, he wasn't in the mood for a confrontation of this nature. Yet somehow he found himself wanting to do something to please her, to make her happy. Hence, he'd talk to these hunters. See what was what and do what he could.

Add to that, if they hiked out of here with these two men, maybe there would be safety in numbers. They had to make it to Gideon. Even if the men weren't willing to accompany them, Zach owed them a warning about the two dangerous men. They should leave these woods and stay clear for a few days, at least.

The two men had stopped and, instead of running away to make an escape, were waiting for their approach.

Realization slowly dawned. It washed over him along with dread. Too late, he saw his mistake. These men were not her poachers. Olivia hiked ahead of him, but the snow slowed her down. Zach used the tracks she'd made to run for her. One of the men cracked a wicked smile.

The other one dropped the doe.

Both pulled out their weapons and aimed.

"Down! Get down!" How many times would he shout those words before this was over?

Olivia slowed to a stop and turned to glance back at Zach—the men ahead of them fired their weapons at the same moment Zach threw himself into her, knocking her into the snow.

He pressed his ear to hers. "Are you hurt?"

Beneath him, she lifted her head slightly and shook it.

That had been much too close. But they weren't out of danger yet.

It had happened so fast, she might not even realize it if she had, in fact, taken a bullet.

God, please let her be okay. Please help us!

No matter if she'd been shot, they couldn't stay here. He grabbed the back of her snowmobile suit, hauled her up with him and, hunkered together, he slid them over behind a tree. Then he fired back at the men to hold them off. Zach had been right to carry an extra magazine, though that had seemed like overkill at the time. He was also glad he hadn't used all his rounds yesterday against these guys.

He faced them again today.

Behind the tree, he took a moment to look at Olivia. She appeared stunned. He brushed the hair from her face. "You okay? You're not shot, are you?" he asked again.

He would look her over completely but he forced his gaze back to the woods. He didn't want to take his eyes from their surroundings too long.

The two men split up. He could see their forms running between the trees. Zach fired at them, forcing them to take cover again. They would probably come around to ambush Zach and Olivia from behind, if he didn't take them out first.

"No, I'm not shot. But I don't understand."

"These aren't your poachers, Olivia."

"But they're wearing hunting clothes. Carrying rifles. The same exact garb my guys had worn. I recognized them."

Their clothes. She'd recognized their clothes. But he said nothing more. He didn't want to think about the reasons why that could be but could see that Olivia was thinking about it. Shock registered in her eyes and on her face. "You don't think…"

Bullets slammed into the tree.

Both he and Olivia ducked. Their eyes locked.

"Stay here and stay down. Don't try to be a hero or try to be strong for me. I'm going to take these men out. But in order to do that, I can't be worried about you. Do you understand?"

She nodded. Averted her gaze.

Zach didn't want to waste another round until he was certain she'd understood. "Olivia, look at me."

Her eyes found his again, the shock slowly dissipating and shifting toward rage at the shooters' audacity, and a visceral emotion that just might save her life—terror. "I promise. I'm not moving from this tree until you tell me otherwise."

Good. She didn't like to take orders, but he could see in her eyes she understood it could mean their lives.

Zach peered from behind the tree again. "I'm going to move so that I can get a better shot. You stay hidden. Dig down in the snow." Which wouldn't be hard. The real trouble came in staying on top of it.

He left her then, trusting that she would be safer hidden next to the tree than with him. Zach hated to leave her, but he wasn't doing her any favors by just sitting next to her like a shield, waiting for the men to trap them. He had to go on the offensive or they weren't going to make it.

Crawling through the snow, he trekked to a patch of manzanita and elderberry bushes, then crouched and ran to a thick-trunked cedar. He lost sight of one of the men, but saw the other creeping his way around. At least he could see *one* of the shooters.

That would have to be enough for now.

Taking even one of these guys out could buy him and Olivia some time and maybe even the real chance of getting to Gideon. The sheriff would want to know, too, what happened to the hunters. Had the shooters killed them and disguised themselves as hunters to draw out their human prey? Or had they simply forced the real hunters to switch clothing and then tied them up in their camp somewhere?

Either way, that strategy had worked. Zach and Olivia had been fooled. But none of it mattered. What was done was done.

He concentrated on watching for his chance.

The shooter crept through the woods unaware that Zach had his sights on him. While he watched the one, he also searched for the second guy, who was probably coming around from the other direction. That's what Zach would do. But Zach couldn't shoot at someone he couldn't see, so he focused his attention on the shooter he *could* see.

This guy might be a distraction to pull Zach's gaze away from the real threat. Once Zach made his shot, he might also give away his position and would need to move quickly if he could.

Inhale...

Exhale...

A few more slow breaths. He focused on the man he would shoot. He wished he had one of their rifles with scopes on them that must have belonged to the hunters. Holding his hands steady, he aimed.

Waited for the shot.

The man slowly crept from one tree, heading for another.

Zach could barely make out his form.

The forest stilled.

Nothing existed outside of the one shooter.

Inhale... Exhale...

Zach fired.

His shot echoed through the quiet.

The shooter dropped.

Zach ducked and pressed into the snow. Now the other shooter would know where to look for him, if he hadn't already. Zach kept low, grateful the snow wasn't as deep in this part of the woods so he could crawl to another copse of trees without too much struggle. A quick glance at where he'd left Olivia told him she was there and remained hidden.

He only spotted her because he knew where to look.

Sucking in a breath, he drew consolation from the fact he'd dropped one of the shooters. Now for the other one. Without getting up, he did his best at reconnaissance to see if he was being watched. The other man might use the hunter's rifle and watch for Zach through the rifle's scope, hunting Zach and Olivia like they were just two deer instead of two people.

Like they were animals.

He couldn't move yet, not until he spotted the other shooter.

God, please let Olivia stay put. Please, keep her safe. I can't let her down. I can't let her down like I let Sarah down.

The memory crushed his heart. He couldn't afford to think of it now, and shoved it away.

And yeah, he'd prayed a lot lately. He hoped it worked. After this was over, he'd need to have that long, heart-to-heart talk with God that he'd avoided for too long.

A jackrabbit dashed away, crossing between Zach and Olivia. Had someone disturbed the small animal? Zach searched the woods. He spotted the glint of metal, much too close to Olivia's position.

Every muscle in his body stiffened. If only he could signal her to keep down.

Don't even flinch.

But she couldn't hear the thoughts he willed at her.

He saw now what must have drawn the shooter's attention—the small bush near the fir under which she'd taken cover shook. That shaking bush gave away her location.

What are you doing, Olivia? You can't afford to move right now.

This wasn't working. Zach could no longer stay where he was and wait it out. The guy would shoot and kill Olivia. He simply waited for his shot. Zach would need to draw the man's attention to himself. But he didn't have a good shot from this position.

He would fire his weapon anyway. That should do the trick.

He sucked in a couple of breaths and got ready to run. It was a risk, but one he was willing to take for her.

Standing, he pushed from the tree and fired rounds as he ran toward where the shooter waited.

A bullet grazed Zach's jacket, slicing deep enough to cut across his skin. He dropped to the ground and crawled forward to a tree.

Another rifle shot rang out.

Olivia screamed.

FIVE

She screamed again.

And wanted to keep on screaming.

She couldn't take much more of this.

She'd run from her hiding place when she'd seen Zach make his own move from the tree, firing his weapon. For her part, she'd been trying to draw the shooter away from him when she'd noticed the man taking aim at Zach. She simply couldn't let that happen. She could see the shooter from where she'd been hiding, but apparently Zach couldn't see him while he tried for the other one.

Olivia didn't have a firearm so she only had one option.

Draw the shooter's attention away from Zach.

By moving the bushes, she'd given herself away. It had been a risk she'd been willing to take in order to give Zach a chance. Besides, if the shooter had taken him out, then Olivia would be left with no way to defend herself.

That gave her an idea.

Since she needed a weapon, she could take the downed shooter's rifle with the scope, along with any other weapons he had.

Olivia had been the one to run after the hunters in the

first place. Her rash decision had caused this trouble. She'd gotten her and Zach into this. She would get them out, despite her promise to Zach to remain in that one spot. At the time, it made sense. But no longer.

Zach continued engaging the shooter, volleys of gunfire erupting through the once quiet forest. The shooter likely had more ammo than Zach. She had to get to the downed man. Was he still alive? If so, then what?

She had no firsthand experience from which to draw.

This entire precarious situation went beyond anything Olivia had experienced, and gave her at least a small appreciation for what Cooper's wife Hadley had encountered with an assassin after her, and when Gemma, Gray's wife, had endured attempts on her life, as well.

How had the two risen above the crises? Had they had any special training?

Well, not Olivia.

She wasn't prepared for any of this. A biology teacher first, she'd traded that to be a wilderness guide—hiking and snowmobiling—which had nothing at all to do with fighting off killers.

She'd better learn fast.

This crash course could kill her.

Olivia would only get one chance at this. She had to hope that Zach would draw the shooter off, or at least prevent him from shooting and killing Olivia.

Her heart rate jacked up. She calculated the path she would take to the downed shooter. When she took it all in, she realized the other shooter was now trying to make his way to his partner, as well. She had to beat him there.

She had to get any weapons he had.

With a glance behind her, Olivia searched the woods

for Zach. His attention was consumed with trying to take down the other shooter.

Then, for some unknown reason, he turned his head and held her gaze. She wouldn't wait for his permission. This was her chance to take action and she needed Zach to understand her plan.

Olivia turned and ran to an enormous white fir.

The round of gunfire that followed told her Zach had understood. She also knew him well enough to know he hadn't approved of her decision. She'd forced his hand. Pressing against the tree, she gasped for breath, white clouds puffing out around her. Would her next breath be her last?

She'd made it this time. What about the next?

The shooter knew where she was headed. He would focus on preventing her. He would try to beat her there.

Panic engulfed her. She wasn't ready to die. Not yet. Why was this happening? She was losing her nerve. Squeezing her eyes shut, Olivia prayed for strength.

Then she heard Zach's weapon firing off rounds. He had given her the chance she needed, using up the rounds he had left, maybe even his last bullets.

With a quick intake of breath, she ran to the next closest tree and then the next.

Closer, she could see the shooter on the ground. Small white clouds from his shallow breathing rose from his face.

He had survived Zach's shot!

If she actually made her way to him, could he prevent her from taking his weapons? Had this been a mistake?

Lord, help me. What do I do?

The question screamed in her head. Indecision could get them both killed.

The more Zach had to defend her crazy attempt to get the guns, the more ammunition he would use, making it absolutely necessary she got to the shooter and took his weapons.

It was too late for second-guessing her decision. Hindsight was twenty-twenty, they said.

Dropping to the ground, she crawled the rest of the way. The shooter would probably pin everything on taking her down before she reached his partner-in-crime.

A bullet whirred past her head and bark splintered from the tree next to her. Olivia pressed her face into the snow, the cold numbing her skin. Unbidden, hot tears burned down her cheeks. Afraid to even lift her head until she had cover, she pressed forward in the snow, sliding across the ground. In the deeper layers, she came to a complete stop. She didn't have time to dig a tunnel.

Another sound terrified her.

The crunch of packed snow beneath boots.

Someone made his way through the snow, coming from where the other shooter had been. She lifted her head slightly above the snow to confirm what she already knew.

It wasn't Zach. No. It was the other shooter.

What happened to Zach? She hoped he hadn't been shot and injured or worse, killed. Maybe he'd simply run out of bullets.

Crunch, crunch, crunch...

He drew closer as fear paralyzed her.

Move. You have to move. Get the weapons before the shooter reaches you. You're going to die if you don't move!

Olivia emptied her mind of any counterthoughts and focused on one thing. Her success or failure would mean life or death. Sliding to the right of her position hunkered in the snow, she bolted to another tree and waited. The downed man lay between her and the shooter on the move.

God, please protect me. Please help me do what needs to be done.

Peeking around the tree, she saw no one at all.

How could she approach the downed man? She couldn't simply walk up to him. Not with the other shooter waiting on her to step out into the open and give him a clear shot.

If only she could communicate with Zach. Make sure he was all right. See if he would help her make this last, mad dash to the downed man.

She sucked in a quick breath and blew it out. Then another. Diving to the ground, she crawled over to the man's body.

Gunfire rang out from behind her. Zach.

He was well and alive! Saving his bullets for when they were needed most.

That confirmed he was running out of ammo. The other shooter must have known it, too.

Olivia scrambled to the downed man and found him unconscious. He'd likely bleed out if they didn't help him. First things first. Keeping as low as possible, she used the man's much larger form as a shield—which would have been unthinkable at one time in her life. Olivia disarmed him, taking the pistol from his limp hand. She removed yet another weapon and ammo from the hunter's jacket.

And then the rifle. She gripped it and slid the strap from his shoulder, then grabbed the box of cartridges from the jacket, as well. She stuffed as much as she could into the pockets of her snowmobile suit, which unfortunately limited her. Then with her hands full, she remained as flat as possible and crawled over to a tall and wide cedar with branches growing close to the ground. Olivia worked herself deep into the cover of the needles and branches, receiving nicks and scratches for her efforts.

She focused on calming her breaths, which could give her away even though she remained hidden within the branches. The shooter had probably seen exactly where she had gone, but he couldn't get a kill shot if he couldn't see her.

Though difficult with cedar branches crushing and pinning her in, she loaded the rifle. With a police officer father who liked to hunt, she'd been drilled on gun safety and how to shoot a variety of weapons. But Olivia loathed hunting. Not in the case where a family needed food, not that. But in the case where people took more than their share like the poachers in the woods near her house who killed the doe.

God, what had become of them?

Likely the same thing that was about to happen to her and Zach if she didn't finish this. After loading the rifle, Olivia inched forward enough to peer through the scope and saw more details of her surroundings.

Zach, where are you?

More importantly, she'd better find the shooter.

Then his terrifying form filled her vision in the scope as he marched through the snow right toward the cedar tree and aimed his weapon.

Out of ammo, he could do nothing more than try to make his way to Olivia. What he dreaded most appeared in his vision. The shooter stomped toward the big cedar tree. Zach's heart jackhammered.

"No! Olivia, watch out!" Zach struggled to run through the snow toward the man. Draw the shooter's attention.

But the man pointed his weapon point-blank at the cedar where Zach had seen Olivia hide. He hadn't been the only one to watch her path.

"Don't shoot!" He tore his way to the cedar, shoving aside deep snow.

He could not get to Olivia fast enough. In time. He was in one of those nightmares in which running toward an object doesn't bring you any closer. Gunfire echoed, the sound of it piercing his mind and heart.

"Olivia!" No, no, no, no… Not again. He couldn't lose someone again. Not someone he cared about. Not like this, especially because he hadn't been strong enough, smart enough, fast enough to save them.

The shooter dropped his arm, and hitched to the side.

What?

He glanced at Zach running toward him, aimed and fired the gun, but his aim went wide.

Realization dawned.

Olivia had shot *him*. She'd aimed and fired her weapon, injuring her assailant. Zach took it all in, his mind slowly grasping what had happened. Then the shooter turned and hobbled away from them. Zach started after him but the cedar branches shook. Had Olivia been shot, too?

"Zach!" She emerged from the branches and threw the rifle down, then ran into his arms. "Oh, Zach. You're okay."

He wrapped his arms around her, so grateful to find her alive and apparently unharmed. His gaze sought out the shooter, but he'd disappeared. Should they follow the man? He dropped his arms and would have done just that, but Olivia stopped him.

"The man you shot," she said. "He's still alive. We need to help him. Do our civic duty. Render aid, if we can, especially since you're a police detective."

Right. He didn't bother to correct Olivia regarding his employment.

They should save another human's life, even if the person had tried to kill them. They should try to save his life from the gunshot wound Zach had inflicted on him. He struggled to comprehend it. The right and wrong of it. Nothing made a whole lot of sense.

Suddenly, out of nowhere, Sarah's voice echoed through his mind from the distant past, calling for his help just before a lowlife shot and killed her. He stumbled forward and almost went down on his knees in the snow.

How many times would he have to relive it in his head?

"Zach, look at me." Olivia cupped his cold, numb face with the soft palms of her hands—she'd removed her gloves—but it was the warmth of her compassionate eyes that brought him back to himself. Images of Sarah, the sound of her voice, faded away until he remembered where he was.

And he looked right into those eyes. There was so much Olivia didn't know about him after a decade. So much he wanted to tell her.

"Are you okay?" She frowned.

He nodded. He'd been a detective. He shouldn't be the one going into shock, reeling this way. But his reaction had been tied up in his grief, his failures, and the reasons he left his job. "You're right. We need to help him."

Olivia dropped her hands away and tugged on her gloves again. Zach remained alert for the other shooter, but the injured man would probably be seeing to his wound for the time being.

Olivia grabbed the weapon she'd dropped and they approached the prone man, who appeared unconscious. "I assume you've completely disarmed him?"

Kneeling next to the man, she looked for his wound. "As far as I know, but he could have a knife or another gun hidden somewhere. I don't think he'll care about anything but staying alive, once he wakes up."

"*If* he wakes up."

Zach weighed his options. He'd prefer to get Olivia to safety. With one shooter unaccounted for, the danger factor stayed high. Once the shooter-at-large had seen to his gunshot wound, would he come back for them or for his partner?

Flakes drifted through the trees and the wind picked up. So much for their reprieve from inclement weather. Zach assisted Olivia in stanching the bleeding of the man's wounded leg. She assembled a makeshift tourniquet from strips they cut from his shirt.

Suddenly, the man gripped Olivia's arm, startling them both.

Yelping, she gasped in surprise, tried to pull free.

Zach shoved to his knees and grabbed the man's hand, prying his fingers from her wrist. The man's brute strength was unexpected.

Face twisted in pain, he blinked up at them. "Please… don't let me die."

"We won't," Olivia said. "We'll try to save you. You're going to be fine, just fine. My house is in these woods."

Did she remember the man had tried to kill her? Olivia had always been softhearted. Zach wasn't sure this was the time for soft-spoken words of encouragement. Their options were few and danger still lurked in the woods. In fact, this man could still be dangerous to them.

"Tell us why you're shooting us." *Where is Rich?* Except Zach didn't want to introduce Rich into the equation in case he'd never been part of it. That small chance remained.

"I'll tell you everything... Just...help me first. If you help me, I'll tell you what you want to know."

So the man would bargain for his life. Smart man.

Olivia's house might be too far for them to carry him. Zach assisted the man to his feet. "Can you walk?"

"I can try." The man lifted his arm over Zach's shoulder and they limped forward. The snow-covered rough terrain of the wilderness wouldn't be much help. When Olivia started to brace the man from the other side, Zach shook his head. "We'll split the weapons. You keep one trained on him, in case he tries anything. And we'll both watch the woods."

Was Zach making a mistake? Would traveling the distance expose them too long, putting them at too much of a disadvantage? At the very least, they had to be quick about it—the other man's gunshot wound could buy them a little time to get to the house and call for help. But it was a risk.

They had only walked a few feet, the injured man grunting with each step on his wounded, tourniquet-tied leg, when a weapon fired off, echoing through the frosted forest.

Zach hurried forward and ducked behind a boulder, practically dragging the injured man with him, who'd suddenly lost his ability to walk.

Olivia had instinctively dropped to the ground and pressed against the snow, as well.

She scooted forward and, once she'd completely hidden behind the boulder with him, she handed the rifle over. “You look for him while I check the tourniquet. I see blood in the snow.”

Using the rifle’s scope, Zach searched the woods, conifers layered thick with white icing blocking his view. Where had the shot come from? Seeing movement in the distance, the shooter shifting his position, Zach fired the rifle. The sound blasted in his ears. Left them ringing. But he remained peering through the scope. The bullet hit the tree and the man ducked behind it. Zach’s shot had been close enough to send the guy into hiding for a few moments while they regrouped.

Keeping his gaze pinned to the scope, Zach scooted close to Olivia and the injured assailant. “Let’s try to get him back to the cave.”

Surprise filled her eyes. “What?”

“It’s closer. We’re too exposed. The other guy stands between your house and us. We’ll never make it.”

“We can’t make it either direction with him shooting at us.”

“I might have more ammo than he does at this point. If I can’t shoot and kill him, I’ll drive him back and away. Then we can go for the cave again. This weather is not going to get any better. We need shelter, too.”

It would be tricky getting the injured shooter up the boulders if he couldn’t walk, but less trouble than trying to make it all the way to Olivia’s house, especially with the other shooter still out there. Once they stabilized the man in the cave, Zach could try to make it all the way down the mountain for help on his own. He could make better time and maybe even get there without drawing the shooter’s attention. On the other hand, he didn’t like leaving Olivia.

Frustration boiled inside. Their options weren’t good.

The man in their care groaned. Olivia checked his tourniquet again. “Zach?”

“What is it?” He didn’t want to pull his gaze from the scope. If he’d had this earlier, he could have taken them both out and been done with it.

Just make your move, buddy. Make your move.

“Zach, I know why I’m still seeing all this blood.” Something in her trembling voice wrapped him in dread.

This time, Zach shifted from the scope and studied Olivia’s expression, his gaze dropping to her hands covered in blood. Nausea churned in his gut. “Olivia… You’re not…”

“No. Not me. The shooter shot his own partner in the back.”

SIX

"He shot his friend, the guy he was working with." Anguish twisted inside as she pressed her hands against the wound on the man's back to slow the bleeding. The bullet remained inside him. She thought of the old saying her mother used. *There's no honor among thieves.* "Was it on purpose?"

"He had a clear shot and could take his time since we weren't shooting back. We weren't hiding behind trees. I think it was intentional."

"Why…why would he do that?"

Zach's eyebrows furrowed. "I think we know why."

He knew too much.

"Why didn't he shoot and kill the two of us instead and come save his partner since he had a clean shot?" The thought of it set her on edge. They'd come much too close to dying today—the last two days, actually. She was ready for a change in their predicament and for the better.

"It could be that he had one shot and killing his partner was priority."

Olivia didn't get it.

"Is he still alive?" Zach gestured toward the man who'd been shot twice now. Once by Zach and once by his partner-in-crime. Zach looked through the scope again.

She checked the man's pulse.

"Well?"

"Yes, but I'm not sure for how much longer." Frowning, she glanced at Zach. "I'm trying to stop the bleeding. Cut me more from his shirt."

They could tourniquet his leg and stanch the bleeding as much as possible, but he could bleed to death internally from the shot to his back, and Olivia could do nothing about that except pray. She would be praying for a bad guy, but there was always a chance for redemption. God gave everyone more chances, and she would pray this guy had another one.

Zach quickly cut more of his shirt and assisted Olivia in wrapping it around the man's midsection.

"You know we could be making it worse, injuring his back more, by moving him."

Sagging, she nodded. "Yeah, but we can't let him bleed to death. And...this changes our plans. We can't make it to the cave now."

"You're wrong. If you were right, then we'd be stuck here because the cave is less distance and trouble than dragging him to the house. So we are going to the cave. And then when we get somewhere and he's stabilized—"

"Stabilized? He's not going to survive if he doesn't get medical attention!"

"What do you want from me, Olivia?" Zach peered through the scope. "I'm doing the best I can."

Olivia could thank that scope for keeping her from having to endure his icy blue, hard stare. Still, it didn't assuage the grief and guilt jolting through her senses. She reached out to Zach, then thought better of it with her bloodied hands. She couldn't wait to wash them clean.

"I know you are. We don't have a lot of choices. At least not good ones."

He stood. "I've lost the shooter. If we're going to make it, we need to go now."

"But—"

"Now!"

Zach slung the rifle over his shoulder and took Olivia's bloody hand and dragged her away from the injured man's unconscious form.

"Wait. Aren't we going to help him?"

"If he doesn't get medical attention now, he's going to die. You said so yourself. We can't help him. Dragging him back to the cave for no good reason only puts us at more risk. This is ludicrous."

Olivia opened her mouth to argue.

Zach cut her off when he pressed her up against a tree, his face much too close to hers. "This man tried to kill you. Would kill you now if given the chance. If he's going to die *anyway*..." Pain edged his features. "You're my priority, Olivia... You."

A knot grew in her throat. She wanted to toss back hateful words. Since when had she been his priority? But she shoved those feelings from the past away. That was over and done. She and Zach were over and done years ago and her unbidden emotions had no place here now.

Olivia thrust her chin out. "We can't leave him. I couldn't live with myself if we left him, could you? We don't know if he'll live or die but he will certainly die if we leave him out in the cold. He begged us not to let him die. We promised we'd do our best."

"We didn't promise. We said we'd try. You said you'd try."

Olivia held Zach's gaze. She wasn't standing down.

"Fine." He stepped back from her then reached down to lift the man up. "I'm not going to carry him in a fire-man's carry. I need my gun hand free."

Olivia took the injured man's other shoulder.

They would have to drag him, then. "I think I've stopped the blood enough so we won't leave a trail to the cave."

Zach didn't respond. Anger poured off him. Well, she was mad, too. Her frustration and disappointment grew with each labored step. The weight of the limp man's form tugged her down. Olivia's muscles burned with effort as they plodded through snowdrifts that fought against them. Biting cold wind that accosted them. At this rate, her burden would pull her down and drag her under before they even made it to the cave. Again…she sighed.

And once they found shelter, what would they do next?

God, please help us. We're going in circles and need a way out of this maze.

Finally, they arrived at the pile of boulders they would need to climb to find the cave entrance. Olivia had no strength left. How would she do this? But determination fueled her.

"Stop." Zach lowered the man against the rocks. Checked his pulse. "He's hanging in there."

Relief washed over her. She realized why she'd been holding on to hope. With everything that had happened, she hadn't been thinking clearly. "If we can get him to wake up, he can tell us why they're shooting at us and more importantly, he can tell us what they've done with Rich, if that's what this is all about. And if he can't, then there's hope that Rich is safe somewhere."

Zach's gaze flicked to her, then to their captive. She couldn't read him at all. He'd shuttered away his thoughts, his emotions. She should be accustomed to that by now. She studied the injured man they'd dragged all this way. At the moment, he was more a mortally wounded captive than a threat.

Lifting the rifle, Zach peered through the scope into the woods for a good long while. Finally satisfied, he lowered it and let the strap hang over his shoulder, then crouched low next to the man. Olivia would have joined him in hefting the man up again, but Zach heaved him up and over his shoulders.

"Lead the way. I've got this."

Could Zach carry the man up those rocks without help? "Are you sure?"

He nodded. She didn't waste time and energy arguing and made her way up the boulders. Zach's grunts competed with the wind in her ears, and the howl of it through the cave as they drew near. Olivia glanced back at Zach and the strain etching his features made her want to assist him, but that could also thwart his efforts and ruin his focus.

"We're almost there." She felt her way around the corner and spotted the small fissure in the rocks. "Over here!"

When Olivia saw Zach coming around the corner and heading her way, she slipped inside the cave, feeling like they had accomplished nothing today. They were back where they started.

Zach followed. She helped him gently lay the man down. She would check his wounds, but could do nothing else. They didn't have medical supplies. The storm prevented her from doing anything else except finding shelter.

The storm and another shooter.

Stretching his limbs, Zach hobbled over to the cave entrance, to stand guard, she assumed. His shoulders had grown broader since she last saw him, and he was much more trim and fit—all this she could tell even though he wore thick winter clothing. He had to be strong to have carried this man up those rocks. She examined the captive's tourniquet and the gunshot wound to his back. When she glanced at his face, his eyes were open, watching her.

Her heart jumped.

"I'm trying to keep you alive the best I can. I said I would, but I can't get you the help you need because your partner is shooting at us. He shot you, too. Why?"

"Doesn't want secrets divulged."

That was as they had suspected. "Where's my brother, Rich? Is that why you were after us?"

Though his eyes glazed over, he nodded.

"And where are the hunters you stole the clothes and weapons from?"

He struggled to answer her.

Zach approached and crouched next to her and the man. "Please, tell us what you know. You said that you would if we helped you."

"Rich wouldn't go along with it. He left the country. We were sent to find him. Kill him and anyone else he told."

Olivia shared a look with Zach. Rich hadn't told either of them his secret, but that didn't matter to these men.

"Is he still alive?" she pleaded.

"I don't know." He croaked out the words.

Olivia wasn't sure what that meant. Had they found him or not? Had they shot him and the man wasn't sure if he still lived?

"Where is he?"

He turned his head. Did he know the answer? She wanted to scream at him.

"He came to see you to tell you—" He coughed and blood drizzled out of his mouth as his eyes found hers. "Supposed to kill you, too."

Olivia squeezed her eyes and twisted her head away.

"What is so important that you have to kill innocent people?" Zach asked.

"Can't let news get out."

The man closed his eyes. Zach grabbed him by the collar and lifted his face closer.

"What news? Rich didn't tell his sister. He didn't tell us anything! Who are you people? We need to know what we're up against."

He was going to die. Did he know that? The man opened his eyes again, nodding his agreement as though he understood they needed information and he would give it.

"Rich, where's Rich?" Olivia had to get that out of him. "Please tell me before it's too late. Before you—"

Olivia stopped herself before she told the man he was going to die.

But he nodded, the understanding of his fate in his eyes. "I'm ready to meet my Maker."

While she hoped that was true, she could hardly believe he would care about a Maker when he was killing people. Her heart wept.

"Rich…" She spoke her brother's name, fearing she wouldn't learn what happened to him.

"Your brother…got…away…"

"But where is he now?"

"Tell us what you know!" Zach's desperation came through loud and clear.

The dying man peered up at him. "Too much is at stake."

Then the flicker in his eyes died with him.

Still gripping the man's collar when he gasped his last breath, Zach felt his stomach clench as he loosened his hold on the shirt. Slowly, he lowered the body. Pressed the lids closed over lifeless eyes. Then Zach shut his own eyes and drew in a long, uneven breath. That had been entirely too traumatic. He'd left his work to avoid these kinds of encounters, especially after Sarah's death.

Olivia...

He couldn't bring himself to look at her. That could render him weak and helpless.

His father's voice blustered through him like the wind through the cave. *"Man up. Take charge of your heart and head, control of your emotions."*

Next to him, she sniffled. Hearing the evidence of her tears magnified his despair. How did he find his friend? How did he keep his friend's sister alive and safe? At least now they knew their lives were forfeit if they didn't discover a way to stop this. That the men had targeted them for a specific reason.

"We'll leave his body here for the sheriff. He's not going anywhere and bringing him with us will slow us down." Though this revolved around Rich, Zach couldn't be sure it involved Rich's job with the contract security firm. It could have nothing at all to do with that. But they couldn't get answers in this cave. His tone sounded far too gruff, but he couldn't help it, though Olivia didn't deserve that from him. He hoped she knew his frustration wasn't directed at her.

"But the storm. And the other shooter is still out there."

"Let me think."

Zach paced the cave. Glanced at the body. Every moment spent stuck in this tomb wasted time. Rich needed them, if he was still alive. They needed to get to the authorities and tell someone what was going on.

Except Rich's words came back to him.

Meet me where we used to vacation. It's urgent. I can't trust anyone but you. Don't let me down, buddy.

They had to be careful what they shared. Zach and Rich had been as close as brothers at one time, but after everything that had happened, they both kept their distance because communicating would only bring them grief, the memories too raw and painful after Sarah's death. Olivia had mentioned the same—she hadn't spoken with Rich in much too long. The tragedy had torn them all apart. Maybe that was why Olivia had moved to the wilderness.

To run from her life. Carve out a new one.

He'd never known for certain if Rich blamed him for Sarah's death. It had been enough that he blamed himself for not being good enough or strong enough to save her.

None of that mattered now.

Focus, man, focus.

After everything, Rich had contacted him—the only person he could trust. Translated: they had to be careful who they talked to. It could mean the difference between life and death.

"Zach?"

He wasn't ready to look at her. He was scared. She'd

see that in his eyes. This was all too much like what had happened to his own sister—Sarah's life in danger because of him. Now Olivia's life had been threatened because of her brother.

Once he gained control over his emotions, Zach turned to her, willing himself to risk a look into her sad eyes. And he saw what he'd expected. Her grief tore through him, but he steeled himself against the tide.

"It's not that far, Olivia. The storm's not as bad as it was yesterday." This time he purposefully kept his voice gentle. That turned out to be harder than he thought. "We can't stay here. If the other shooter finds us here..." He wouldn't finish the brutal thought.

"The snowmobiles or the house?"

He shook his head. "I suspect the guy who died was probably military, Ex-marine or ex–navy SEAL, it doesn't matter. He said the stakes are too high to let their news get out. Now that I have a better understanding of this situation I know that we cannot go back to your house. If I were the shooter out there, I would have taken up residence in your house. Or sabotaged it. The same for the snowmobiles. They knew Rich had gone to the house and thought he'd come to see you and tell you what he knew. If I understand correctly, they knew you were living in that house before Rich did."

Olivia slid to the ground and leaned her head back against the hard rock wall. "If we're hiking all the way down to Gideon in this storm, I want to rest for a minute."

Good idea. They had a long hike ahead of them.

Zach would do the same. Take a minute to get warm and rest his legs. He moved to stand in front of her and looked down. "I'll give you two."

How she managed a soft smile he didn't know. He

almost wished she hadn't. He sat down next to her, but not too close.

"I've been thinking about something," she said.

"Yeah?"

"If Rich had gotten away even for a short time to recuperate, to see to his wound, I know he would have come to this cave. I just know it."

Zach nodded his agreement. Though they hadn't seen any evidence of that. "And?"

"Well, to think it all through logically, he probably would have known that I would then be involved in all this since the men followed him here. And he would have tried to communicate with me in the only way left to him."

"And that is?" Zach wasn't sure where she was going with this.

"He would have left something for me in this cave. We loved playing in here growing up. We played cops and robbers, spy games, cowboys and Indians. And we left clues that we scratched in the wall."

"So you want to look for a clue?" He hadn't meant for his tone to be so incredulous. They both needed sustenance. Maybe she wasn't thinking clearly. Zach considered that a far-fetched idea, but he would humor her. "Okay, then we'll look for a clue."

She climbed to her feet, leaving him sitting there. Now that he'd taken a moment to rest, the adrenaline that had kept him moving started to crash. Not good. Zach rubbed his face. He'd give himself another minute or two as they searched, skirting the body in the cave.

After fifteen minutes of searching, Zach took her hand. He'd wanted her to find that clue if it would help them resolve things and find Rich. But more than that, he didn't know if he could stand to look at her disappointed face.

And when she looked up at him, he'd been right to dread this moment. Pain etched her features, and hopelessness filled her eyes. "It's not here. I thought… If it's true and he got away then he would have come here. I was certain that Rich would have left us a clue. Something. If it's here I'm missing it. It could be staring me right in the face and I don't even see it."

"Don't be so hard on yourself. Rich wouldn't make it that difficult if he'd left a clue."

"Now I don't know what to believe. Where to turn."

Covering her face, she *did* turn to Zach. Pressed her face against his chest.

Their lives weren't the only thing on the line. If he didn't resolve this soon, his heart wouldn't survive.

SEVEN

"What if he's not alive? What if he's already dead? Oh, Zach." Tears choked her throat. "I can't bear the thought."

Overcome with despair, with the possibility her brother hadn't survived, Olivia could no longer hide her vulnerability from Zach. She hadn't the strength to fight it and gave in to the racking sobs she'd restrained through the brutal hours since this nightmare began.

Though she'd held on to hope, she realized that doubt had pervaded her thoughts. Realized how much she'd counted on finding Rich before now, finding him in the cave.

And just beyond her grief, she heard Zach's soothing tones, felt his strong but gentle hands rubbing her back. "He's alive," Zach said. "You have to keep believing he's alive."

She dropped her hands from wet cheeks and wrapped her arms around him, pressing her face into his jacket, his shoulder—the natural thing to do. A small part of her wished he'd remove the thick winter wear so she could get closer, but she felt his warmth all the same.

And he responded, his arms bringing her in for a tight embrace. Beneath his jacket she could feel the strength in his arms and chest. The strong back that had carried the dying man all this way and then up the rocks and into the cave. The strong man who'd kept them both alive, protected her from two military-grade killers.

The tendrils of attraction swirled up from her toes, woven with memories of their past love. What was she doing? She couldn't even embrace this man she'd let go of long ago without going right back. Olivia unwrapped herself from his arms and stepped away. Unable to look him in the eyes, she averted her gaze.

But he didn't let her move far before gently reaching for her hand. "We have to believe he's alive, hope and pray that's the case, but...I don't want to give false hope here."

"I know, I know." She didn't want him to say it. "I need to prepare myself for the possibility that he's out there somewhere, lying dead in the snow." A sob choked out.

"Just because you didn't find a clue here doesn't mean he didn't come to the cave to regroup, maybe patch up his wound and move on. He covered his tracks so they wouldn't find him and that's why we can't see the evidence he was here. If he's alive, he'll find a way to Gideon to contact the authorities and send help for us."

"No. If he was going to contact the authorities, he would have already done it. Maybe he doesn't want this to get into the wrong hands, like he said when he contacted you. In that case, he won't send anyone to find and save us."

Zach frowned. She read the look in his eyes.

Not even for his sister?

"If not, then he'll find a way to communicate. In the meantime, we have no choice but to leave the cave and try again to escape this mountain. But this time, we have more ammo and you have a weapon, too. There are two of us against one."

"Maybe. Unless he went to get more men. Who knows? But even if it's two of us against the one, you said he's military, or ex-military like Rich. Like the men in the contract security company he worked for. I'm not sure we have the skills to combat that."

Studying her long and hard, he released a sigh.

She'd hurt him and that hadn't been her intention. "Zach, you have the skills. You're a law enforcement officer sworn to protect. I trust you."

An indefinable emotion flashed in his eyes, then, "Glad to hear it."

But she heard the doubt in his words, saw it in his demeanor. He didn't truly believe she trusted him. He carried the memories of the experience that had cost him Sarah around with him. It was more that he didn't trust himself.

Turning his back on her, he hiked over to the cave entrance holding his gun, always clutching his weapon. She understood. He had to be prepared for the worst-case scenario—the other shooter finding the cave. He'd made it clear protecting her was his priority.

Olivia stood over the body of the dead man. Looking down at him like this was morbid, she knew. But this man had tried to kill her, Zach and Rich. "The sheriff will probably want us to come all the way into Gold Beach to give a statement. But Zach, if we figure out where Rich is, then we don't have time for that. Maybe we can call the sheriff and tell him where we're headed and if it's out of his jurisdiction, he could have connections and send backup. Or the Oregon State Police. You're a detective. Will that help us? Or cause us problems?"

Since her father had been a police officer, she understood sometimes law enforcement entities could bristle when others tried to function in their capacity out of their region, even with proper authorization. Then again, they could get their help much more quickly because of it. Politics. Always politics.

"Liv… Olivia!" He'd used the name he used to call her when they were together a decade ago.

Nobody else had called her Liv. "What?"

"You're getting ahead of yourself. Let's focus on one thing and one thing only. Getting to Gideon without dying."

"Not until we agree on a plan. I don't want any confusion about what we're doing when we get to town. This is my brother we're talking about."

He stared out the opening. "I hope the storm lets up soon. We need a break."

He was putting her off while he thought it through. She knew that much about him. Zach had changed and there were attitudes and mannerisms she didn't recognize, but in more ways than one he remained the Zach she'd known. He would measure his words now, and once he'd said them, there would be no changing his mind. She hoped he would agree with her.

Olivia inhaled and waited.

Finally, he glanced at her. "When your brother contacted me, he made certain I understood the urgency and that he couldn't trust anyone else. And the information the shooter told us seems to confirm that. There could be important people, powerful people, behind this news he mentioned. Was it that Rich couldn't go along with the plans to hide things? Some mission gone wrong, or high-stakes game? I don't know, but he left them and they followed him here to commit murder. It's that big. I don't know if he was going to turn whistle-blower or not, but he intended to tell at least one person."

"And that was you."

"Right. But there's more."

"And that is?"

"Before we head out into the storm, there's something you should know."

He hadn't wanted to tell her. To even bring it up. If only there was another way. But she counted on his connections in law enforcement the same way that Rich had. Except telling her might dredge up everything he'd wanted to avoid. Both of them needed to forget.

Focusing on the storm outside, he noticed the wind had died substantially and the snow was no longer a driving force, but flakes drifted lazily. Crazy weather was the norm.

They should leave now.

But first, the truth. "I resigned. I'm not a detective anymore. I have no official connection with the Portland PD." He'd been such a disappointment—and embarrassment—to his father that the man had taken early retirement. After Sarah's death, Zach had lost his confidence. Couldn't focus. Couldn't get the job done. It had taken him three years to admit it. He left shortly after his father. Hard to believe he hadn't been in law enforcement for a year now.

Unable to watch her expression as she took in his news, he kept his gaze fixed outside. He could let the snowfall mesmerize him, wait for her response. Talk it through. But no point in explaining. If Olivia knew anything about him, she would understand why. "It's time to go."

Trusting Olivia to follow, Zach stepped from the cave and continued his escape from that solitary confinement to which they'd been forced to return. He didn't want to see those walls again. Before he started the climb down the boulders, she caught up with him, seized his arm, tugged him around. Forced him to look at her.

"You quit? Why?"

Her question wrenched his gut. He thought she would understand how much Sarah's death had affected him. But maybe it had been much too long since he'd had a connection with her. She didn't know him anymore. Had forgotten that being a police officer had been everything to him, and losing his sister because of that had devastated him. But he'd fooled himself. Zach tried to forget why this news would also affect Olivia. He'd lost her because of his dream, too. He'd chosen his career over her. Only unlike Sarah, Olivia had been free to choose, too. Free to live out her life.

"It doesn't matter," he said. "We have to hurry while the storm has let up. And we have to watch for the other shooter. He's still out there. We don't need the distraction of a conversation. You understand that, right?"

Her frown deepened and her warm eyes reflected disappointment, but she nodded. He'd seen that same disappointment in his father's eyes. Zach turned away from her and started down the rocks. The sooner they got to Gideon, the better. Though once they made it to town, this would still be far from over. Above him, Olivia yelped. He glanced up in time to see her slip and fall toward him. Bracing himself on the rocks, he caught her legs then let her drop down into his arm. Flakes landed and melted on the warm skin of her face.

"Are you okay?" he asked.

"Yes, thanks." Admiration flickered in her gaze. "I don't know what happened."

He shook off his surprise and set her down next to him, secure on the boulder. "You're tired and hungry. Same as me. All the more reason for us to get somewhere warm and safe. Get some food in us."

When they'd descended the boulders, Zach used the rifle's scope to search the woods. Seeing nothing out of the ordinary in the quiet, pristine forest, he believed it safe to keep going, but he kept Olivia right next to him. "Which way is the shortest way down?"

"The shortest way isn't the easiest and could be dangerous."

"What do you recommend then?"

"I'm up for it, just wanted you to know it isn't a simple walk in the woods."

Once a path was agreed upon, they hiked through the snow, sometimes waist-high, which drained his energy reserves faster than Zach would have thought. Adrenaline kept them alive and moving. Climbing down more boulders, and complicated, snow-covered terrain. Though they progressed, Zach's extremities quickly grew numb with cold. Olivia squeezed his arm. He glanced at her, fearing that he would fail her, too. That they weren't going to make it out of this alive. Maybe the shooters hadn't gotten them, but the cold wilderness would.

"We're almost there, Zach. We made it."

If there was one thing he knew, the last two miles were the most dangerous. But he let his hopes rise, if only a little, and picked up the pace. He could smell the aroma of something delicious sizzling. She was right. They had to be close. The scent of smoked meat set his stomach rumbling. A rush of adrenaline had him practically dragging

Olivia behind him. He'd rented his snowmobile in Gideon, so had been in town recently. Now he'd have to explain why the machine remained up in the mountains—the least of his worries.

Through the firs, pines and cedars, a few scattered homes appeared. Beyond those, log cabins and nostalgic architecture for the tourists made up the bulk of the buildings in the community. The sound of vehicles and snowmobiles—civilization—was music to his ears. Olivia took the lead as they slid down a snow berm and got their footing on the street.

They'd made it! Zach struggled to believe their good fortune. Finally...they'd gotten a much-needed break from their nearly two-day trauma.

"Where to?" he asked. She knew the town.

"Wilderness, Inc. I need to tell Cooper, my boss, what's happened."

"Your boss? Are you sure that's the first person you want to talk to?"

"He's a friend, too. He'll know what to do. We can call the sheriff from there."

"Remember, for your brother's protection, we don't want to divulge too much of the situation. We need to find him first."

She hiked forward. "But we need to tell the sheriff about the shooters and the man in the cave. About the two hunters who are possibly hurt—or dead. But what about Rich? We'll have to tell them the shooters are after Rich, won't we? I'm not sure. And I don't want to jeopardize his life."

His friend's words swept through him.

Meet me where we used to vacation. It's urgent. I can't trust anyone but you. Don't let me down, buddy.

Zach didn't want to let him down again. And if keeping his secret until they knew more would save lives, Zach had an obligation to keep this to himself.

"No. We tell them about the shooters and that's all. I haven't decided how I feel about a SAR team searching for him if he made it off the mountain and is hiding somewhere else. Let me talk to the sheriff and get a sense of him."

Rich had put too much burden on their shoulders.

Still, Zach had made the wrong decision about his sister. "It's your call, though, Olivia. If you think there's a chance he could be hiding in the woods up the mountain, wounded or otherwise, we need to tell them."

She shoved her fingers through her hair, pushing it back from her face that was red with cold. "I don't know. I can't know."

"Just remember that every person we tell is at risk. I'm afraid of the collateral damage if we involve more people. Rich didn't trust anyone, so we need to trust him in this—that he found a way to escape the shooters. A place to hide. And he's waiting on us to find him. But if we tell someone else, even one person, his location could leak to the wrong people. And those wrong people will go there and kill your brother. Wait there and kill us."

Olivia visibly shuddered. He fought the desire to reach out and bring her close. Hold her and protect her.

Zach didn't like the idea that Rich had gone off and left his sister, but maybe he thought he was leading the shooters away from the area. Or maybe he knew Zach was on his way and would protect her. Why? Why would he trust Zach to protect Olivia when Zach hadn't been able to save his own sister—Rich's fiancée?

But this wasn't the time to be second-guessing what his friend had done.

They hiked through town. With each step, his boots grew heavier. Olivia slowed, as well. The weight of their burden along with two days of fighting to stay alive, weighed on them. He wanted Olivia to stay behind, somewhere safe and secure, while he searched for Rich.

But he knew what her answer would be. She would insist on searching, too.

Come on, buddy, where are you? Let us know something.

So that would mean they would go together. He would be responsible for protecting her. Zach hadn't asked for this, any of it. But then neither had Olivia.

She stomped up the porch of a house. A big window allowed him to peer inside. A sign hung outside the door.

Wilderness, Inc.

She put a lot of trust in this man, Cooper Wilde.

Who was he to her? More than simply her boss?

And why, after ten years, did Zach care? He realized then that he'd tried to protect his heart from external factors—proximity to Olivia Kendricks and how she affected him—when this whole time, he should have been guarding it from the inside where little cracks were forming, letting what he still felt for her leak out.

He'd never wanted to be in this position again. He hadn't been able to bear the responsibility anymore after Sarah's death, so he'd quit his job.

And now here he was again.

Keeping people he cared about safe was harder than he ever could have imagined.

EIGHT

God, please let Cooper be here. Please let him help.

Olivia turned the knob and stepped through the door into the house that served as the Wilderness, Inc. storefront. Six sets of eyes looked up from the table at the back.

Cooper rose from his chair. "Olivia, what's happened?" When he looked at Zach, his gaze narrowed.

She rushed forward and would have spilled everything, but Zach's voice behind her broke through, cautioning her.

"Can we speak in private?" she asked.

Her boss nodded, then looked at the people around the table, all of them watching with interest. Olivia wanted to tell Alice—Cooper's sister—a woman she considered a close friend, but Zach had warned against sharing the information with too many people.

And Olivia absolutely couldn't be the reason another person was hurt.

Cooper led the way into his office in the back. Olivia entered, followed by Zach, and Cooper shut the door behind them. He took a seat at his desk and gestured for them to sit on the sofa in the small room.

"I haven't been able to raise you on your radio or SAT

phone at the house. We were just discussing taking some snowmobiles up to check on you and your brother."

"When I left you, I headed straight to the house and—"

"Excuse me, but who is this?" Cooper eyed Zach.

"Oh, I'm sorry." Olivia would have started the introductions, but Zach stepped right in.

"I'm Zachary Long. An old friend. You can call me Zach."

Cooper zeroed his gaze in on Olivia. "Is that true, Olivia? Is he an old friend?"

She frowned. "Yes, of course."

Her boss relaxed. "Just want to make sure. You show up here looking like you've been through something awful with this stranger next to you."

"I was just here yesterday and rented a snowmobile from your outfit. I talked to someone… He wasn't at the table."

"That might have been Tildan. Now, tell me what's going on."

"When I got back to the house, I saw that Rich had taken off on a snowmobile. I followed his trail, and the blood."

"Blood?"

Zach shifted next to her. Apparently he didn't want her to share even that much. Was he crazy? This was her brother. Though she'd wanted to keep the sensitive information to herself until they knew more, it was much harder than she'd imagined.

Tears leaked out the corners of her eyes, but she kept her voice steady. "Then Zach showed up and two other men shot at us."

Again, Cooper eyed Zach, his distrust apparent.

"I'm not the bad guy here." Zach had noticed, too.

"No, he saved me, Coop. If he hadn't been there,

I don't know what would have happened. Zach had a weapon and fired back at them. We ran and holed up in a cave. Then this morning we tried to escape but they were waiting on us, dressed like hunters—the ones I've been telling you about. I recognized them right off."

"And she took off running and yelling at them." Zach cut into her story.

Cooper nodded. "That sounds about right."

"Only it wasn't my hunters. It was those same shooters. They did something with the hunters. Took their clothes to fool us."

Holding up his hand, Cooper reached for his phone. "I think this is a story you should tell the sheriff. The hunters could be dead or wounded. And we need to find your brother. We need a SAR team up there."

Olivia nodded. "Sure, go ahead and call. And we left a dead guy in the cave."

Cooper had already called the sheriff and was waiting. He stared at her, his gaze shifting between Olivia and Zach. "And the dead guy is?"

"One of the shooters." Zach stood, thrusting his hands into his pockets.

"Something tells me there's more to this."

Olivia stood this time, anxiety cording through her. "Look, Coop, my brother is still out there. Zach and I are going to find him. This is a dangerous situation."

"We don't want to say anything else." Zach caught her gaze and held it.

Cooper's expression said everything, but he spoke into the phone to the sheriff's department, and brought up the two hunters and Rich, her brother.

When he ended the call, he stood. "Sheriff Kruse is

coming as soon as he can get free. An SAR team is being organized for the hunters and your brother."

"Wait, Coop."

"What is it?" He studied Olivia.

"I'm hoping… I'm hoping that Rich is alive and he got away so that would mean he's not in these mountains, I don't think. We don't want anyone else to get hurt. The shooter is still out there."

"Maybe not," Zach said. "They were there to kill Rich and anyone else in contact with him. We're here. And if Rich made it out, too…"

"There's one way to know if he got away."

Olivia drew in a breath, realization dawning at the same instant Cooper spoke.

"He rented a snowmobile from us. His vehicle would still be parked in the lot up the road unless he got out some other way."

She bolted to her feet and started for the door.

"Hold on." Cooper spoke in his take-charge voice. "I'll check on the vehicle. Do you know what car it is?"

"No… I… He didn't tell me. He'd only come in the day before."

"We'll figure this out."

"Look, Cooper," Zach said. "We haven't eaten since this started. We're exhausted. We need rest and food."

Cooper stood and edged his desk then opened the door. "Since you're not willing to tell me everything, and that's fine, I'll let the sheriff figure this out. In the meantime, you can use my old apartment above us to clean up, Zach. And Olivia, I'm going to send you over to Alice's. You can shower and rest and get some grub."

"What about the sheriff?" Zach asked.

"It'll be a couple of hours before he can get here. Might

as well clean up and rest while you wait. In the meantime, I might be called out for the search and rescue." He led them back to the table.

"Zachary Long, meet Alice Wilde, my sister, who works with me here at Wilderness, Inc. Melanie Shore, our friend and coworker. My brother, Gray, and his wife, Gemma. They run a wildlife conservation organization that works to save big cats in their natural habitat."

"Which in turn preserves habitats and ecosystems," Gemma interjected.

"Yes. That." Cooper chuckled at Gemma's expected passionate response. "And this is my wife, Hadley."

His gaze shifted to Alice. "Can you take Olivia with you over to your place so she can shower? And feed her, too."

"Wait." Olivia got their attention. "This is… I don't want anyone to get hurt because I'm here. Because we're here. Men are trying to kill us. I don't want to tell you more, but they think we know something, some secret my brother brought back with him from the Middle East. But we don't know anything at all."

"Olivia." Zach's tone warned her not to say more.

She'd changed her mind and disagreed. "They need to know what they're getting into by helping us. It doesn't matter if I tell them anything or not. You and I know nothing and yet someone is trying to kill us anyway."

Pursing her lips, Alice stood. "Come on, Olivia. Let's get you over to the house where you can eat something and rest until the sheriff gets here. Gray and Gemma can hang out with us and help keep watch in case these men show up. Gray used to be a federal special agent with the Fish and Wildlife Service. He can protect us."

Olivia flicked her gaze to Zach. "And Zach used to be with the Portland PD."

Zach subtly stiffened. Why had she said that? It wasn't anyone's business, but she'd wanted to lend him credibility, given Cooper's obvious distrust.

Alice, Gray and Gemma led Olivia a few unconventional blocks down to a log cabin situated a hundred yards back from the main buildings that made up the very small historical town of Gideon—or rather, unincorporated community—sitting in the middle of the Wild Rogue Wilderness. In the summer, tourists came for the fishing, white water rapids, camping and hiking. And in the cold-weather months, winter sports, including snowmobiling.

But Olivia had come for the peace and quiet.

Once inside the familiar and cozy dwelling, Alice showed Olivia to a guest bedroom with bath and brought her clean clothes. Olivia took a long, hot and glorious shower, and when she finished, found a bowl of hot beefy stew and homemade bread on the nightstand next to the bed.

That Rich hadn't found a way to communicate disturbed her. She'd missed something. That had to be it. But she couldn't think things through clearly on an empty stomach or without rest, so she started in on the stew.

Zach insisted that Rich claimed he couldn't trust anyone other than Zach. Asking the wrong person for help could be detrimental to them all. But what to do? She couldn't think when she was so hungry.

Olivia quickly finished off the food. With her belly full, exhaustion pulled her down onto the soft bed. All she'd wanted was to create distance between her and the pain of the past, and to start a new life. Even though the family vacation home held its share of memories, those memories bore no resemblance to the trauma of the recent years. Living in the Siskiyou Mountains and working for Wilderness, Inc. had helped her to move on.

But that plan had now backfired. Drama and tragedy had followed her here. She was in danger, both physically and emotionally.

A soft knock came at the door and Alice peeked inside. "I don't want to disturb you, but I need to ask you something."

Rubbing her eyes, Olivia shifted to sit up in bed. "Sure, what's up?"

Her friend sat on the edge of the mattress. "Cooper wanted me to ask you. And now that I have you alone… Is this man Zach a danger to you in any way? Are you under any kind of duress?"

An incredulous laugh escaped. "No, Alice…just…no."

"Are you sure? You don't have to be scared. We'll protect you. Cooper thought it was strange he showed up along with the men shooting at you. You seem uncomfortable with him. We don't know the whole story and it doesn't make total sense."

Olivia rested her head on the pillow again and stared at the ceiling. "Zach and I were in love ten years ago. I would have married him. He and Rich were best friends. He's here because Rich called him to come, claiming Zach was the only person he could trust. Because of Rich, Zach is in danger, too. He kept me alive and protected me. I feel safe with him." And the last couple of tortuous days, he'd been everything that she'd always known he was—strong, brave and yeah…selfless.

Alice released a long breath. "Okay. You've convinced me that he's safe. I'll leave you to rest and wake you when the sheriff arrives. Cooper is gearing up to go with the SAR team up the mountains to the cave and the areas you detailed."

When Alice left the room, Olivia tried to sleep, but her thoughts wouldn't let her.

At one time, she'd called Zach selfish for giving her up like he had. But Olivia keenly felt the brunt of her mistake. She'd been the one to give him up just because he needed to be the man he was—a police officer. A detective like his father.

Olivia had been the selfish one. Her selfishness had cost her Zach. They could never go back to what they once had. Unfortunately, seeing this ordeal through would mean sticking with Zach to find Rich. She'd have to keep her emotions in check.

A few minutes later the soft knock came at her door again. Olivia hadn't been able to sleep as much as simply rest in the bed.

Alice peaked in. "The sheriff's here to question you."

Olivia tried to shake off her exhaustion and hoped she and Zach told the same story.

Zach pulled a T-shirt Cooper Wilde had loaned him over his head, eager to scarf down that stew Cooper's sister Alice had made. Homemade bread, too. Olivia had done well for herself settling in near Gideon with a job at Wilderness, Inc. Looked like the people here were not only her coworkers, but good, caring friends. Almost like family.

They appeared protective of her and suspicious of him. As he finished the last bite of stew—and wished for another serving—he could almost smile about that.

A loud knock came at the door. "It's Cooper."

And now he could expect to be grilled.

When he opened the door, he was surprised to see not only Cooper, but his brother, Gray, and the sheriff. The three men stepped into the living area of the small makeshift apartment in the house converted into the Wilderness, Inc. business.

"Zachary, meet Sheriff Kruse," Cooper said.

The sheriff extended his hand and Zach took the beefy hand attached to a stocky man in his sixties. He held the air of someone who'd been around the proverbial block a few times. Zach wasn't sure if that would help him or hinder him.

"I'm heading out to help search for the hunters." Cooper stood at the door. "And to locate the body in the cave. I'll let you share the details with the sheriff."

"But I'm staying," Gray said, and he shut the door after Cooper stepped out.

Zach noticed the continued suspicion in the man's eyes. He supposed he couldn't blame the Wilde family—after all, he was a stranger—but the two brothers were taking it a bit far where Zach was concerned.

"Have a seat." Zach gestured to the sofa, though it wasn't his apartment or his sofa.

Both the sheriff and Gray eased onto the black faux leather, and Zach took the wooden chair at the table.

"Have you already talked to Olivia?"

"Yes. Now I want to hear your story."

Zach should have expected they would split them up to hear their stories, even though they weren't the criminals here.

"How's she doing?" He understood this experience had to have traumatized her. He'd been in law enforcement and he was feeling the effects himself, no matter how he tried to control his unsteady limbs.

"Alice is taking good care of her," Gray said. "Olivia is probably sleeping now. Don't worry. You should know that she's like an adopted sister to us. She was pretty broken when she first showed up in Gideon, and we took her in. She attends church with us. Eats Sunday dinner with us, and a whole lot more. Works with us all hours of the day and night. It's just the nature of our business to grow close to each other. So in the last two years she's changed a lot. Seemed happier. But then you show up—that, and the look on her face when she walked in today, and it was like the last two years never happened."

Right. Blame this on Zach. "Look, you have this all wrong. While I'm glad she found a way to move on after all she's been through, I didn't even know she was here. I didn't come looking for her or deliberately bring trouble to her door."

"All right now, let's get back to your story. Time's wasting." Sheriff Kruse shifted forward on the sofa. "Tell me what happened on the mountain starting with why you were there."

This was the part Zach felt uncomfortable about. How much should he tell the sheriff about Rich's phone message? He'd just stick to the basics for now. "Olivia's brother, Rich, and I go way back. We all do. But I haven't talked to Rich in a few years. I knew he'd been working in the Middle East with a private military contractor—a security firm. Some big company."

"What do they do, exactly?" the sheriff asked.

"His company outsources ex-military types to provide protection, guard facilities, act as security for VIPs and their convoys, perform crowd control. You name it."

The sheriff nodded. "Go on."

"A few days ago he left me a message to meet him up at the vacation house. I spent time with his family here when we were kids. So I headed this way. I rented a snowmobile, but when I got to the house, nobody was there. So I followed the tracks out back, and that's when I came across Olivia. I hadn't expected to see her there. We were just going to head back to the house to call for help in our search for Rich when the gunfire started."

Sheriff Kruse nodded, taking it all in. Zach had a feeling about this sheriff. So he told the rest of the story just as it happened, despite his earlier misgivings about telling the sheriff everything. Had Olivia done the same?

"And what about Rich's message? Did you get any sense of urgency? Like he was in trouble?"

Nodding, Zach held the sheriff's searching gaze. He got the sense he could trust this guy. "He told me that I was the only one he could trust. He said it was urgent. And here I am telling you, when he trusted me to keep things to myself."

I'm sorry, my friend, I'm sorry. But things had gotten out of hand.

"You can trust us, Zach." Gray pushed to his feet and paced the small space.

"Olivia hopes he got away." She was still hanging on to the hope he'd left her a clue as to where.

"And it's probable she's right. His vehicle—a green Subaru Outback—is gone. I know that because only two people rented snowmobiles in the last two days. That's you, Zachary Long, and Rich Kendricks. He paid cash but I got his driver's license information for the rental. So now the question is, where would he go?" Gray asked. "Why would he leave Olivia to face the men trying to kill him?"

Zach bristled. He needed to find his footing with these two men. Just what dynamic was at work here? "Who are you to ask the questions?"

Sheriff Kruse laid a hand on Gray's shoulder. "He used to be in law enforcement. He cares about Olivia and the people of Gideon. Just answer the questions."

That's right. A special agent with FWS. But not anymore. Still, he doubted the reasons this man left law enforcement had any similarities to Zach's reasons. "I suspect he wanted to draw the shooters away. And maybe he did draw them. There could have been more than two. Or maybe he's dead on the mountain, the killers took his vehicle, and Olivia is hanging on to false hope."

There. He'd said what he hadn't wanted to admit for her sake. And for his own. He hung his head, rubbed his hands together to warm himself against the sudden cold that slipped into his heart.

A brutal cold that he had to fight at every turn.

God, please let Rich be alive out there somewhere. Please help us find him and keep him safe. Keep us safe. Please keep the SAR team and the people searching for the hunters safe. Help them to find those men well and alive.

He said the silent prayer, but he couldn't bring himself to believe any of it would be answered. At least not the way he wanted.

The sheriff stood then. "I think I've heard everything I need to know. At least the storm's let up and that will give the SAR team a chance. I'll start the search for Rich's vehicle."

"What about the other shooter, Sheriff? Are you worried he's still out there and might cause problems?"

"Everyone has been warned and they're armed. My deputies are with them, as well. I've pulled all my resources to focus on this. Let's hope we find the hunters alive and well. Maybe they've been bound and can't get free. We might wait until morning to retrieve the body from the cave. Just depends how everything plays out."

Zach saw in the man's eyes that his words were just that—only words. With what the sheriff had heard he didn't seem to believe they would find the two men who'd been poaching alive. Maybe they'd been breaking the law, but they didn't deserve to die for their particular crimes.

Gray opened the door for the sheriff and said goodbye, but he didn't follow him out. He shut it then leaned against it and crossed his arms.

"I hear that you and Olivia used to be a thing. Circumstances have thrown you back into her life again. She's been through enough. Been hurt too much."

"I already know all of that, probably more than you do." Much more. He couldn't see Olivia sharing all the sordid details, especially if she had tried to build a new life here.

"Yeah, well, we don't want any repeats."

Bristling again, Zach rose from the chair to face the man. "Who are you to talk to me about Olivia?"

"Like I already said…she's like a sister, an adopted sister. Or did you not hear that part? From what I saw, she looks pretty bruised up on the inside again. I'm wondering if that has more to do with your sudden appearance back in her life than it does with these shooters after her brother and now the two of you."

Yeah, there was that possibility. Seeing her again had affected him far more than he'd like. Zach scratched his jaw.

"The shooters we faced were professionals. Military-grade. So I'm wondering, if you're here and Cooper's gone with the SAR team, then who's watching over Olivia while she's sleeping? Your wife and sister?"

NINE

Olivia opened her eyes.

Where am I?

Heart fluttering with panic, she tried to remember. Soft orange light flickered, creating shadows that danced across the wall.

Oh, that's right. Alice had offered her guest bedroom.

Olivia watched the dancing shadows for a few seconds, then she rose up on her elbows with a slow dawning as she looked at the southwestern-styled wallpaper border with geometric shapes. She'd left the cave feeling like she'd missed something. Their drawings as children. She remembered them clearly now. After twenty years, she hadn't paid much attention to the drawings or the cave so, exhausted and hungry, she hadn't recognized Rich's clue when she saw it. When she'd stared right at it.

The last shape at the bottom—it had to be new.

That had to be Rich's clue.

Olivia scrambled out of bed and flicked on the closet light. Inside she found the extra clothes Alice had been kind enough to put in the guest closet for her. Her friend had given her several choices. She let herself smile at that. Quickly, she dressed. She had to find Zach to tell him the news. Tugging on a pair of jeans that were only slightly big, she found a turquoise T-shirt, then pulled on a Nordic sweater.

When she turned off the closet light, she again noticed the orange light filtering through the window and into the bedroom. Her breath hitched. She hurried to the window to peer out.

Flames. That was no light but a fire!

Someone banged on her bedroom door. "Olivia, wake up!"

She hurried to unlock the door and opened it.

Alice rushed in and grabbed her shoulders, her voice excited. "There's a fire over at the barbecue place." Looking Olivia up and down, she added, "You're dressed?"

"Yes, I…"

"Good. The volunteer fire department is in Gideon. Most of us are unofficial volunteers."

"Of course. I'm glad to help."

"I don't know if there's anything you can do, but I don't want you to be here alone so do you mind coming with me?"

"Of course not." In fact, Olivia enjoyed feeling like she was part of a community.

They grabbed coats, hats and gloves and donned their boots. "I take it Gemma and Gray are already out there?"

"Yes."

"What about Coop? Is he gone with the SAR team?"

"Right again. But I don't know about your Zach—if he'll be out there."

Olivia didn't bother correcting Alice. Zach wasn't hers. Still, this was the perfect opportunity for her to find him and tell him she believed she knew where her brother, Rich, had gone to hide. They had to head there as soon as possible. "If not, maybe I'll get him."

She wasn't sure if Alice heard her as she opened the door, letting snow swirl inside. Together they rushed out into the night and chaos. Olivia hurried to keep up with Alice as she maneuvered, cutting through the Douglas firs and ponderosa pines for the shortest route. A crowd had gathered around the business, flames engulfing one side. Male and female volunteers dressed in firemen suits and hats with masks stood next to the idling fire truck tanker that carried a big tank of water—two thousand gallons, she'd guess. Not everyone helping wore the official VFD garb, though.

She shivered in the cold and wrapped her arms around herself. Weird there'd be such a big fire in the middle of the winter with all this snow on the roof that quickly melted into water under the intense heat.

"Stay here." Alice waited for Olivia's reply. Once she nodded, Alice stepped into the melee near the fire truck and spoke with several men who appeared in charge.

Though Olivia stood more than twenty yards back, she could still feel the heat coming off the flames as she searched the crowd for Zach. She was eager to tell him about the clue, but it was more than that. She wanted to see him to make sure he was okay. If she knew anything about him—he would be in the thick of things, helping the volunteers, but she didn't see him, which worried her.

A few volunteers hung back on the other side in the shadows. Olivia inched her way between the people gathered. The fact the crowd appeared rather large surprised her, given the small town with only a few businesses and structures. Apparently, they'd come out of the woods—

literally—to fight for one of their own. Besides, Ricky's Rogue Bar-B-Q was practically a town icon.

On the other side, she didn't find Zach but she spotted Gemma. Her husband Gray stood a few yards from her and actively managed the fire hose along with a couple of other guys, directing water to the flames. Olivia slipped between the warm bodies of onlookers to Gemma's side, and tugged on her coat sleeve.

Gemma turned to look at Olivia, and spoke loudly to be heard over the roar of the flames, the idling truck and the water hose. "Hey, what are you doing?"

"Alice came out to help. I'm looking for Zach. Have you seen him?"

Gemma shook her head. "No. He's probably catching up on rest, which is what you should be doing. You need to go back to the house and stay there."

"Alice said she didn't want to leave me alone, so I'm out here with what looks like the whole town."

Pursing her lips, Gemma searched the gathering, presumably for her sister-in-law. "Wait here with Gray. See that lever? Shift it to the right when he gives you the signal. I'm going to find Alice and bring her over."

"Wait, no!" Olivia protested, but Gemma had already disappeared into the mass of faces reflecting the glow of flames.

She felt like an idiot now. When Gray looked over his shoulder and spotted her, he arched a brow behind the visor. She shrugged in response.

An explosion shook the ground. Olivia braced herself and the flames soared higher. The crowd screamed and ducked. Some scattered.

What was going on? Was an explosion normal? Gray stood his ground, dousing the flames. Olivia's gaze caught the gauge on the side of the truck. The water stores were quickly depleting and still the flames blazed. She hoped the community had a plan B.

A burly man wearing fireman gear stepped up next to her and looked her up and down. Then he gestured to her position next to the lever. "You should have suited up. But I got this now."

Olivia had no reason to doubt him so moved away from the lever. She spotted the Wilderness, Inc. house down the street. Maybe Zach wasn't aware of the fire, since the apartment was situated in back of the house. He could be sleeping through all of it like Gemma said. Olivia didn't want to wait until the morning to tell him the news of the clue, and she was absolutely certain he'd want to know the information immediately. He'd want to be part of this scene. To avoid this situation in the future, they needed to make sure they got communication devices—cell or SAT or radio, she didn't care which.

She left the crowd and trotted down the snowplowed street. The closer she drew to the house, the more her stomach fluttered at the thought of seeing him. Why did he still affect her like this after ten years? But she knew why—this older Zach was like a new improved version in every way. Except he appeared colder and harder, too, but that had come with his position as a police officer and then promotion to detective. She couldn't fault him for those characteristics that had only made him stronger. She would have smiled as she hurried toward the house, but her attraction to the man was no smiling matter. She couldn't go through the pain or risk of love again, and pushed those thoughts away.

At the door, she turned the knob and found it locked as expected. How could she reach him up in the apartment? She banged on the door, and still got no response. Then she remembered there was a direct entrance to the apartment in the back.

Hurrying around the house, she found the stairs up to the apartment. With the weight of her foot, the first step creaked. A chill raced through her.

"Zach!" she called up at the window, hoping he'd hear and wake up.

She gripped the railing to run up the steps and drew in another breath to yell Zach's name.

A hand clamped on her arm and yanked her down the steps. Another hand covered her mouth.

Zach dragged her into the shadows and against the vinyl siding of the house.

Olivia kicked and fought.

"Sh… It's me." He hadn't meant to hurt her but there'd been no time for gentleness.

Against him, she stiffened. "I thought—"

Too loud! He pressed his hand over her mouth again. Then slowly, she relaxed, seeming to understand there must be a reason for his actions.

And there was. The shooter had come looking for them.

Was up in the apartment now.

He leaned in close to her ear and caught the scent of smoke and strawberries from her hair. "The fire," he whispered, his voice barely audible, "was only a distraction."

He'd gone searching for her and missed her everywhere he went. And then when she called his name, he ran around the house and spotted the curtains in the apartment above moving. There'd been no one in the house when he'd left, and he was certain no one would come into the apartment except to find and kill him.

The angle of the stairs prevented the person inside from seeing her on those bottom steps. When she'd been about to shout a second time, she approached that next step. Zach thought he'd been quick enough when he'd grabbed her and pulled her out of the assailant's line of sight.

He hoped and prayed.

Leaning back, she angled her head toward him and whispered. "What now?"

He wasn't sure. There wasn't any law enforcement in the town to speak of—the sheriff had gone off to assist in the search for the hunters, but even if he hadn't, he didn't usually stay in Gideon. And practically the whole town had come out to see to the fire at the barbecue place, a tourist attraction and likely the best restaurant in Gideon.

The door above opened and closed quietly. The guy must have chosen to come out the back and down the stairs because he'd heard Olivia calling for Zach.

Doubting they would go unnoticed in the shadows, Zach braced himself for a fight. And like an idiot, he'd left his weapon up in Cooper's apartment. Gently he urged Olivia deeper into the shadows and behind him.

Surprise was his only advantage.

The moment came quicker than he expected.

The man bounded down the steps and when the bottom one creaked, his gaze swung around as though he sensed their presence. His eyes locked with Zach's. Lunging at him, Zach kicked the weapon out of his hand before he could bring it around.

Then he faced a muscle-bound fighter who gripped

his throat. Zach used every technique he could think of to get free.

Get air.

His pulse roared in his ears.

Black spots dotted his vision.

In his periphery he saw Olivia approach. His mind screamed for her to run, to get away. She swung a board against the side of the man's head. His grip loosened and he dropped to the ground.

Zach sucked in air, tried to get his footing. "Thank you," he croaked.

She gulped air, puffing out white clouds. "We got him."

Before they could detain him, the man scrambled to his feet and darted into the woods.

Zach ran after him.

"Zach, no!" Olivia yelled behind him.

But he ignored her. He'd been stupid to let the guy get away, but the man had recovered from the knock to his head quicker than Zach would have expected. Zach plowed through snowdrifts and into darkness. He couldn't let this guy get away and come back for them later. They would be looking over their shoulders until this was done.

As he pushed deeper, his eyes adjusted to the glow of the inferno that illuminated this part of the woods in soft orange light. He followed the tracks and then found two sets of them. Clearly, the guy had come down the mountain from the same direction in which he'd run away. Zach needed a flashlight and gear. He turned at Olivia's approach.

Breathless, she leaned on her thighs to catch her

breath, holding the guy's weapon in one hand. "I was trying to bring this to you. But we lost him already."

"Nope. Didn't lose him yet. It's not snowing. His tracks should lead us right to him. But I need light to follow him and that could also give me away."

"I'm glad to hear you don't plan to chase after him."

"I'm glad to hear you have so much confidence in my abilities."

He hurried back down, hiking in the tracks already made. Grabbing Olivia's arm, he tugged her behind him as he went.

"That's not what I meant. I'm just… I'm just worried about you."

Something in her voice, some nuance of emotion, had him stopping in his tracks and turning to face her.

"I don't want to see you get hurt, that's all. I couldn't stand it if something happened to you."

He wanted to melt right into those warm cinnamon eyes suffused with compassion and an emotion he'd best steer away from. He didn't need this right now. Her turning soft on him. He didn't want it. Maybe he lied to himself on that point, but it was all he could do to focus on keeping them alive.

Swallowing against the sudden lump in his throat, he grabbed her hand again and returned to hiking back to the house. He'd tell Gray about the tracks and maybe together they could hunt this guy down. And this time, he'd make sure Olivia stayed behind somewhere safe. To think the shooter had remained in these woods when the SAR team was out there somewhere unnerved him. Zach hoped no one would run into him.

"Wait," Olivia called. "I can't keep up."

He hesitated in his tracks then finally faced her. The

orange glow of the fire—which was now beginning to die—highlighted the gold in her copper hair. His breath hitched.

He didn't have time to wait. But this was Olivia, and he'd do anything to keep her safe. He'd do anything for her at all, like give up his dream this time, if he had that to do over again. But it was too late for any of it. Why did these unbidden thoughts continue accosting him?

"I hate to admit it, but I'm not in as good of shape as the rest of these Wilderness, Inc. people," she said. "Not yet. But I'm working on it."

"You're doing great, Olivia." Not just anyone could have survived the ordeal they'd endured. But it hadn't destroyed Olivia. No. It had just made her stronger and more determined. And that would be a problem regarding Zach's next words. "Listen, I have to go after this guy before he kills someone else. Now's my chance."

"You can't go."

"I *am* going and you're not. I'm hoping to take Gray and some of the others. We also need to communicate with the SAR team to let them know he's alive and well."

"That's not what I mean." She stepped closer.

Zach seemed to be having trouble understanding Olivia tonight. "What now?"

"I know what the clue is, Zach. I know where Rich is hiding. That's where we need to go. We need to make sure he's safe. Let the others get this guy still on the mountain."

"What are you talking about?" His mind scrambled to remember, to track with her. "What's the clue, Olivia?"

"A diamond."

TEN

Olivia wasn't sure she appreciated the incredulous expression on Zach's face.

"A diamond?" He gently urged her forward so that they cleared the woods and neared the town again.

"Sh. You said that too loud." She looked over her shoulder into the woods. The dying fire still illuminated the forest, golds and reds dancing off the tree trunks. "I don't want him to hear."

"He's long gone. Making his escape. He knows I'm coming back for him loaded for bear." He held her shoulders. "Now, what's this about a diamond?"

"I knew there was something I was missing when I looked at the drawings in the cave. I couldn't believe they were still there after all this time. But something about them bothered me. Then I woke up in the middle of the night and the wallpaper in Alice's guest bedroom is a southwestern pattern with diamonds. That's when I knew what was bothering me. There was a diamond added to our drawings. It was plain as day, but I just didn't recognize it for what it was."

"How is a drawing of a diamond going to help us?"

"Come on, let's talk about this inside." Olivia closed

the distance between them and the house and hiked up the stairs. Zach hesitated, obviously uncertain if she truly had something to go on or if she was wasting his time.

Finally, he followed her up and opened the door for her. Flipping on a light, he let her in and glanced around the apartment.

"What is it?" she asked.

"I don't know. Maybe the guy left an explosive for us here. I hate that he always seems to be two steps ahead of me at every turn. But keep talking while I search the place."

She wanted his full attention. He wasn't taking her seriously. "Zach!"

He came out of the bedroom, his eyes wide. "What, Olivia? What happened?"

"You're not listening."

Zach strode toward her, then lifted her hands and held them just like he used to. "I'm sorry. I wanted to make sure it was safe. Now, tell me about the diamond."

Though gloved, she could still feel the current from his hands flash up her arms. Olivia stepped away. "Diamond Lake. He's at Diamond Lake."

Zach's icy blues studied her. "You know that because you saw a diamond drawn in the cave."

That incredulous look again.

"Yes. I know it." Well, maybe it was only a very strong guess. "Even if I'm wrong, we can't ignore the clue. We have to go there to check it out. See if we find Rich. And we have to go tonight."

"I'm going back up the mountain for that shooter and I'm taking Gray Wilde. He used to be a special agent. He can help me."

"Forget the shooter. He's after Rich. Others might be, too. We have to find him first."

Zach shed his gloves and scratched his head. Ran his hand over his jaw. "And then what?"

"What do you mean?"

"I would think Rich would have gone to the authorities by now since people are trying to kill him. But you really think he's at Diamond Lake?"

"He did go to the authorities, in a manner of speaking, Zach. He contacted you, remember? He thought you were in law enforcement. But regardless, we haven't heard from him. If he'd gone to the authorities—FBI or police or whoever—we would have heard from him by now. So that must mean he's hiding at Diamond Lake."

"Except even if he'd gone to the authorities and tried to contact us, how would he reach us?" he asked.

Olivia shed her coat and gloves, too, his meaning dawning. "We don't have phones, you mean."

"That's what I mean."

"He would have sent someone to check on me. He could have called the sheriff or Cooper's office here and sent someone to find and help us, too. No, Zach. He's at Diamond Lake. It's all we've got." Olivia did something she never wanted to do, but this was her brother. She stepped close enough to Zach she could smell the musky scent of him mixed with smoke from the fire. "Please, Zach. Please. Go with me to Diamond Lake. Help me find my brother."

He hung his head. "You don't have to beg me. I never meant for you to have to beg. I'm here because Rich called me to help him. Of course we're going to Diamond Lake." He looked up at her then.

Goose bumps ran over her arms. She remembered that look and it took her back fifteen years. They were both still in their teens. She had such a huge crush on him.

He scrunched his face.

"What's wrong?" she asked.

"If Rich didn't call the sheriff, even to check on you knowing those guys were out there, that means he didn't want anyone to know. Not even the sheriff."

"And we told him." She hung her head.

"What we knew. But something's not right, Olivia. I can't imagine he would have left like that."

"I think he probably wanted to draw the men off. I know Rich. Maybe he didn't know they would try to kill us, too, but at least he could draw them off."

"Well, it didn't work," he said.

"That doesn't mean he isn't alive and out there hiding, waiting for me to show up at Diamond Lake. Waiting for us to show up there so he can tell us this big secret that has him scared to death."

"You're probably right. If I know anything about him, he loved his sister."

Shame filled her. She loved Rich, too, and yet they hadn't spoken in far too long. She'd blamed Rich for so much—for the loss of their mother. They'd needed him to come back to the States, if only for a while. But that was in the past. Olivia was forging a new future just as soon as she found her brother.

"Tonight. We need to go now before anyone asks where we're headed."

Nodding, he grabbed his coat and gloves. Glanced at the window. "Sun's coming up, so tonight has already gone. Let's get out of here. I'll find a way to call your friends and tell them we're heading out so they won't worry. I'll let Gray know about the man still up in the mountains so he can tell the sheriff. I parked my truck up in the lot for the snowmobile rentals so we can drive that, but we have to hurry before anyone notices."

"And you still have your keys?" Olivia thought they'd just about lost everything except the weapons they'd confiscated and then left with the sheriff for evidence, though Zach still had his own weapon.

He yanked the keys out of his pocket and tossed them in the air, catching them again. "Yep. But my cell phone is somewhere up on the mountain buried in the snow."

Zach opened the apartment door to the steps out back. Someone knocked on the other door that connected the apartment to the house. Olivia shared a look with Zach.

He pulled out his weapon and leaned against the wall next to the door. "Who is it?"

"It's Gray."

Zach relaxed, but only a little. They had wanted to escape before anyone realized they were gone. He opened the door. Alice and Gemma stood next to Gray. Soot and grime covered all their faces.

"May we come in?" Alice asked.

Zach opened the door wider. Olivia stood back out of the way. She sensed something was coming. The three stepped into the apartment.

"Looks like you're going somewhere," Gray said.

Olivia gave a vague nod. Zach said nothing.

Alice and Gemma moved to Olivia and hugged her. "We didn't know where you'd gone."

"We thought we'd lost you."

"I'm sorry to worry you. I went to find Zach."

"The sheriff radioed." Gray cut through the niceties. "There was no body in the cave."

What could that mean? Surely they didn't think she and Zach had made the story up. No, that couldn't be it.

Olivia glanced to Zach, but he stared straight on, keeping eye contact with Gray.

"But there was a body in Ricky's Rogue Bar-B-Q," he added.

A body?

Zach didn't see blame in their eyes, but he couldn't help but feel guilty—after all, they'd brought this trouble to the town of Gideon. Still, what else could they have done but come here for help? "I'm sorry to hear that. Was anyone able to identify the body?"

Inwardly he cringed. If the body had been burned, his question might have come across as insensitive.

"Oh, no, please don't let it be..." Olivia cried.

Zach did the only natural thing he could do. He wrapped his arms around her. His gaze found Gray's in hopes the man would understand his silent question.

Did the body belong to Olivia's brother, Rich?

"It's not Rich, Olivia." Gray twisted his face up. "Why would you even think that?"

She stepped out of Zach's arms as though she suddenly remembered herself. "Then who is it?"

"We don't know." Alice frowned. "But we're hoping you can tell us."

Time for Zach to speak up and say what they were not saying. "So you guys think the fire might have been set by our shooter."

"Yes," Gray said. "We don't know for certain it was the man after you, but there had to have been an accelerant to fuel that blaze."

Gemma held her husband's hand. "We were worried when we realized it might have been a distraction to get to you."

Zach slipped his hand over Olivia's shoulder and squeezed, wanting to reassure her. "You were right. He was here in the apartment. I chased him into the woods."

"We were going to tell you about him so that you could warn the sheriff and the others." Olivia reached up and put her warm hand over Zach's.

He could see the touching didn't go unnoticed by the Wilde family. Stepping next to her, Zach dropped his hand. How were they going to get out of here now? They'd wanted to make their escape before anyone could stop them.

Gray paced the small space. "If there wasn't a body in the cave, and the other guy was here, then I wonder if the body we found in the fire was his buddy. The accelerant and the explosion was not only a distraction, but could have been meant to get rid of the body. If we don't even know who the guy was then dental records won't do us any good."

Zach's stomach clenched. "So the body was burned that badly. How can you be sure that it's not someone you know?"

"He's burned but not completely. Bubba was determined to save his late father Ricky's restaurant and found the guy and pulled him out. It's no one from around here, unless it's a tourist. But he looked military, like you said. Add in that he has gunshot wounds..." Gray eyed Gemma, Alice and Olivia. "I'm sorry, ladies. I hope I'm not getting too graphic here."

"All the more reason I need to find my brother." Olivia glanced at Zach, her only warning that she was giving away their plans. "I think I might know where Rich is hiding and we need to get there. We were just leaving when you knocked on the door."

Angry lines carved into Gray's face. He opened his mouth to speak.

Olivia cut him off. "Please, Gray. What if this was Gemma, Alice or Coop? If there was a chance you could find them you would have already left."

Studying Olivia and then Zach, he nodded. "Where do you think he's gone?"

That was where Zach would draw the line. "We don't feel at liberty to share."

"What do you mean?" Alice asked. "Why not?"

"Rich was very specific that he couldn't trust anyone," Olivia said. "In fact, we shouldn't have told the sheriff as much as we did, but under the circumstances, we had no choice."

"So you're saying he can't trust the sheriff? The police? What could…is he in some kind of trouble?" Gray put his hands on his hips.

"I don't think that's it, at least not in the way you mean." Zach pulled Olivia with him as he inched closer to the door behind them. "This situation must involve his contract security work and people in high places. People with power and means to send killers across the ocean. People who don't want some secret revealed or some mishap exposed."

"So if the wrong people find out," Olivia said, "then Rich, Zach and I could fall into the wrong hands. It could mean our lives, Gray."

The man, the former special agent, didn't appear convinced. Zach didn't care.

"If it's so dangerous, you go alone." Gray gestured at Zach. "Why involve Olivia?"

Sucking in a breath, he wanted to agree—

"This is my brother. I'm going and you're not stopping me. You can't keep me here. I need to find him and make sure he's okay."

And somehow make up for the past. She hadn't said the words but Zach could hear it in her voice. Those were his thoughts, as well.

"I'll keep her safe, don't worry." He could tell by the way she stiffened he'd said the wrong thing. Why was he giving those reassurances? Had he forgotten his failure with his own sister?

"I don't need a protector. But if you don't believe that, know that I'm safe with Zach. There's no doubt there."

Her confidence in his abilities, despite his failure that had left Sarah dead, squeezed his heart. His doubt in his own skills could get them both killed. He had to see this through with her, for Rich's sake, if not for Olivia's. But yeah, this was for Olivia's sake more than Zach would like to admit. He wanted to see that smile in her eyes again. And so he shook off the self-doubt.

He would protect her to his dying breath.

Her heavy sigh drew him back to the moment.

"You guys keep safe, too." Unshed tears in her eyes, Olivia put her hand on the doorknob. "I'm sorry about Ricky's Rogue Bar-B-Q. If we hadn't have come—"

"No." Alice tossed Olivia a half smile. "Don't even think like that. Bubba's wanted a new, bigger kitchen for a decade. This will give him the excuse he needed to get one."

"Just what are we supposed to tell the sheriff when he shows up and asks for you?" Gray's tone was accusing.

The sheriff had his hands well and full and there was a good chance this would all be over before he even thought about Olivia and Zach again.

Zach pressed his hand over Olivia's and turned the knob, opening the door to freedom. "You can tell him anything you want."

ELEVEN

Olivia climbed into the passenger side of Zach's blue Silverado pickup. The cab was cluttered like always. He hadn't changed much in that regard. But familiar smells filled the inside and wrapped around her, sending memories crashing down on her again. Memories that were almost too much to bear, especially when he got into the truck on the driver's side and peered at her with his icy blue eyes.

Déjà vu.

An easy smile started on his lips but quickly morphed into a thin line. "You should know that I'd prefer leaving you here in Gideon with your friends where I can trust you'll be safe. Taking you with me to find and help Rich isn't my idea of a great plan."

He stared as though still waiting on her to change her mind.

"Considering the guy found us here, I'm not all that safe if I stay, and I don't want to bring more harm to this town or my friends."

Frown deepening, he started the ignition. The truck rumbled to life. Olivia stared out the window at Gideon, wishing the scenery could chase away the images of her riding with Zach in his truck when they were just teens. But nothing could stop the memories and familiar feelings of first love that made her heart dance in anticipation.

Her breaths were unsteady, and she hoped Zach hadn't noticed. Somehow she had to push it out of her mind. She glanced at him, watching him navigate the plowed road through town, steady and self-assured. Somehow she had to let him go completely. How was it possible that she had never truly done that?

Once the truck warmed up, Zach switched on the heat, letting it blast through the cab.

"I don't know about you, but I didn't get much rest last night. Why don't you sleep on the drive?" Zach maneuvered out of Gideon and onto the one road out of town. "We don't know what we're going to find once we get to Diamond Lake. We have a long day ahead of us."

"I'm not sure I can rest until we get off this road. The drive is treacherous even without snow and ice." Though with warm air that wrapped around her like a comfy blanket filling the cab, she might struggle to stay awake.

"You'll just have to trust me." He glanced her way then back to the road. "Do you trust me?"

"Sure. You know what you're doing."

But had there been more to the question? Olivia sensed there was, but maybe it was her own traitorous imagination. She was glad he was forced to concentrate on the road because she couldn't hold his gaze. Instead, she watched out the window, admiring the beautiful snow-covered forests of the Wild Rogue Wilderness.

Sure, she trusted him. But Olivia couldn't trust herself. She couldn't trust her own heart to be with this man on this dangerous mission without growing soft on him again. It seemed impossible that she was in this situation. Forced to be in proximity to a man she'd loved so completely, but apparently not enough to let him pursue his dream.

A car came into view in the passenger window. "Do you think he'll follow us?"

Zach looked in the rearview mirror. "Sure, the car behind us will follow. This is the only road out."

"You know what I mean. The bad guy. The man trying to kill us and Rich."

"Even if he tries, we can lose him before we give away our destination."

"I hope you're right." But seeing even one vehicle behind them made her nervous. "I hope we actually find Rich there alive and unharmed. But obviously he didn't escape unscathed."

"Before he worked contract, he was in the military. They're trained on how to treat themselves and survive. Remember? I wouldn't worry about that. There are greater threats on his life. What bothers me now are the shooters who tried to kill us. Are there more of them? Do they already know where Rich is? I'm sorry to bring that up, but we have to consider the possibility that even if he escaped, they might have found him and he's already gone, Olivia."

No. She couldn't think like that. She had to hold on to hope. "Maybe the guy in the apartment last night just wanted to stir up the town to see if we'd show up so he could, in fact, follow us to Rich. He could have killed us. We didn't even know he was there."

"True. This man is definitely determined."

And that had her terrified. "It's hard to imagine that someone followed Rich halfway around the world to kill him for what he knew. Part of me wants to run away from it. To stay as far away as I can from all this. But he's my brother and I can't do that. Not this time." She'd told him more than she wanted. Let him see too much. And hadn't she escaped into the wilderness to leave behind the drama that loving others could create? But here she sat next to the man who had broken her heart. She had no control over her life.

"Is that the reason you moved here to the old vacation cabin? To…escape?" He cleared his throat. "But you've built a new life for yourself. You did well. I'm proud of you, Liv."

Proud of her? What was she supposed to say to that? *Thank you, and please don't call me Liv*? She kept the words to herself.

But his question…his question, she couldn't ignore. And she answered it with one of her own. "Why are you suddenly getting personal?" Maybe it wasn't possible for them to be together for so long without talking things through.

"I don't know. If you'd rather not talk about it… It's just that Gray said you were in bad shape when you showed up in Gideon and they took you in as part of their family. I'm sorry for everything you've been through. And for my part in it." His voice shifted and cracked on the last word.

"Zach, really, there's no need to apologize. Life happens. And you're right, I moved out here to get away from too much tragedy. I know you've suffered your share, but it overwhelms me how much I've lost when I think about it too much. At the cabin I find good memories, and a fresh landscape with new friends and, yeah, a new family of sorts. But now I even regret that because I lost

Rich, somehow, and I might never get to see him again if we don't find him alive. That's why I need to see this through to the end with you. I have to find him."

Tears choked her words but she forced them down. "And what happened before with Sarah's death, Rich staying overseas, and Mom's fatal car accident, that's one side of it. The other side is about what happened before, with you. And I've sworn off love for good." Now why had she gone and brought Zach into it? But everything built up inside and was ready to explode. He'd opened the lid with his question. Might as well finish the obvious issues they danced around.

"For good." He said it like a statement instead of a question.

Zach slowed the truck as he steered on the outside lane where the scenery took her breath way. From the treacherous edge of the road, she could see the length of the canyon, jagged ridges and dramatic outcroppings surrounded by old-growth forest. She had to remember to breathe.

"For good—or forever—is a long time to swear off love, Olivia." He was back to her long name now. "I don't see it happening, myself. You're young and drop-dead gorgeous. Strong and independent."

"Stop. Just…stop it!" She didn't want to hear the compliments, especially coming from him. They only served to break away more of the wall. "So what about you? I don't see a ring on your finger. Are you married?"

He swerved a little hard and the back end almost fishtailed. "Nope."

"Have you ever been married?" These days, one never knew.

"Nope. But I almost got married once. There was this one girl…"

"Why are you doing this?" She covered her face.

His hand pressed against her arm and forced it down. "Aw, I'm sorry. I was only teasing. Trying to lighten things up. We're spending some time together. And I don't know about you, but I can't handle being serious all the time. I can't handle stepping around what was between us before like it never happened. I want to move past all that, don't you? When this all started, I said that what was past, was past and we could handle it, but I haven't been doing so well. I thought maybe you were struggling, too."

He stopped the truck at a turnout to allow a faster-moving four-wheel-drive go by. That gave him the chance to stare her down with his icy blues that were far from cold. "Was I wrong?"

Olivia couldn't look away. A rush of emotion surged inside, sweeping her away. She couldn't let that happen, but she couldn't lie to Zach either. He would see the truth even if she tried.

I'm struggling with your nearness, too. I'm struggling with how I used to feel for you.

"No, you weren't wrong."

Her eyes—those big beautiful eyes—held him captive. Why had he dared to ask that question? Knowing the answer, especially with the longing he saw in her gaze now—would surely undo his resolve. Being done with love for good—he understood her need to protect herself from the pain.

All he'd wanted was to lighten the mood and move to the next level with her—to friendship without the whiplash of first love gone wrong between them. But his question had the opposite effect.

Zach lifted his hand and cupped her cheek, before he even realized he'd done it. Then he couldn't move his hand away from the soft skin of her face. "Okay, so we're in this together. And we both know where we stand. But we can see this through, Olivia, for Rich's sake."

She closed her eyes and he thought she would lean into his hand, but she pushed back against the door, her head against the window, breaking the connection.

He let his hand drop.

"Why did you quit? You loved law enforcement. You made detective. It was your dream."

In her words, he heard more questions— *Why did you give me up for that if you were only going to quit?*

That wasn't something he could easily answer.

Time to pull back. Zach eyed the rearview mirror, checked traffic and then steered onto the road once again, giving himself time to answer that question.

"I mean, if you don't want to talk about it, then don't." She tossed his words back at him.

He'd been the one to broach a sensitive topic. She probably still dealt with the pain of him choosing his career over her.

"It's not that I don't want to talk about it. Why I resigned… It's just complicated and I haven't worked through things yet, even after a year. I don't know how to explain it." He'd told her the truth, but more than that, it was still far too painful.

"I hope it didn't have anything to do with Sarah. That wasn't your fault, Zach. You did the best you could do."

He banged the steering wheel, releasing his frustration that way so he wouldn't take it out on her. His best hadn't been good enough. After his father had resigned, Zach had known it was his time to go. Everyone in the department had known that before he had realized the truth. He needed a good long break before he could ever work in law enforcement again.

"Oh, Zach." Olivia put her hand on his arm.

Where she touched him burned and he wished she would drop her hand, but he understood she tried to reach out to him, comfort him. He couldn't reject her.

"It's okay. Like you, I'm trying to start a new life for myself." Funny that he'd landed here with Olivia in his truck all over again. Life could be so ironic. "If I had it to do all over again—" Was he really going to say this? "If I had it to do all over again, Olivia Kendricks, I wouldn't have taken the job. I would have stayed with you."

Even though at the time, he'd thought she hadn't loved him enough, he was the one who'd refused to understand what she'd been through, and didn't want to go through again. But now, watching her go through this ordeal after she'd moved to get away from the tragedies and start over, he finally got it. He finally saw it clearly. He'd lost his sister and it had crushed him so that he couldn't even stick with his job. He understood Olivia so much better now.

Since her father had been killed in the line of duty, she hadn't wanted to devote her life and love to Zach only to lose him like she'd lost her father. How blind and arrogant could he have been? It was like a punch to his gut.

She dropped her hand. "I think we shouldn't talk about this anymore. I'm going to try to sleep, if you don't mind. Like you said, we have a long day ahead of us."

Great. He'd gotten too serious when he'd only meant to air things out and move on. But maybe that happened when you were trapped in a situation with a woman from your past you had never really gotten over. But he shouldn't worry. Nothing could ever happen between them again. Like Olivia, he was done with love. For good.

She folded up her coat to create a pillow and stuffed it behind her head next to the window. Her soft snores told him when she'd fallen asleep. Cute. He was glad she was getting much-needed rest.

Once they left the back road to Gideon and hit the freeway where he would connect with the highway to Diamond Lake, Zach pulled in to refuel. He hadn't seen a vehicle follow them out of the wilderness region. Olivia used the facilities and bought them drinks and snacks and cheap burner cell phones, which they plugged in to charge in the truck.

On the road again, neither of them said much at all, but it was still a comfortable silence. While Olivia appeared caught up in the scenery, Zach continually watched the road to make sure they weren't followed. The drive to Diamond Lake traveled alongside the Rogue River as it flowed from Boundary Springs out of Crater Lake National Forest. They traded the Siskiyou Mountains for the Cascades, part of the Pacific ring of fire volcanoes, and the view was nothing less than stunning.

Having the most beautiful woman in the world in his truck, along with the magnificent scenery, could easily distract Zach.

He hadn't had to work this hard to maintain his focus in a long time.

"Okay, so we're getting close. The lake's just up ahead." He finally broke the silence. Beyond the lake was white-capped Mount Thielsen, "the lightning rod of the Cascades" with its spirelike peak, and below the tree line, white-frosted Douglas firs and ponderosa pines surrounded the base like a Christmas tree skirt. The mountain looked as if it had suffered a landslide on one side.

Olivia shifted in her seat. “We should try the lodge first. I don’t know what else to do. The diamond was all I had to go on.”

“It’s okay, Olivia. You did well to try. You’re right—it’s all we’ve got and you know your brother better than anyone. So you think he’s staying in the lodge?”

“I’m not sure. If he is, then wouldn’t the people after him be able to track him there?”

“Not if he used another name. I guess we’ll find out.” He steered into the parking lot at Diamond Lake Lodge.

When Olivia moved to open her door, he cautioned her. “Let’s sit here for a few minutes. See what’s what.”

He’d hoped they would make it here without a hitch, but at the same time, something about this didn’t feel right. That sixth sense he’d learned to heed as a detective told him to expect trouble.

While Olivia was desperate to find her brother…

Zach was desperate to keep them alive.

TWELVE

Olivia itched to get out of Zach's truck. Her search for Rich had consumed her thoughts on the drive. Better that than all the confusing vibes coming off Zach. Yet another reason to scramble out of his truck.

"Can we get out yet? I don't see anything out of the ordinary."

Just the usual tourists here to experience the pristine nature, or what was left of it after the snowshoers, skiers, and snowmobilers had their fill. Still, the lodge wasn't all that crowded in the middle of the week.

"I've got a bad feeling about this." Zach had put on his sunglasses to knock the glare off the snow and peered past her through the passenger window. "Something feels off."

"We're here, Zach. What do you want to do?"

"If he's using an alias then how do we find him? We can't just call up the lodge and ask for him by name."

"Since he left that clue, he knew we would come for him here." She hoped.

God, please let me be right. Please let us find him here—well and alive.

And if he wasn't here, then what? Olivia wasn't sure

what she would do. How she could handle losing someone else. Hanging her head, she squeezed her eyes shut.

Zach's hand covered hers. "We're going to find him. It's going to be okay."

Something in Zach's tone drew her gaze up to his. Some emotion completely foreign to her lingered in his eyes. She'd always thought the icy blue color of his irises emphasized Zach's goodness and honesty. His transparency. But not anymore. She couldn't read him at all. "What is it? What's bothering you?"

"Nothing." His brows furrowed, then he seemed to shake it off. "This is what we're going to do. You're going to sit in this truck and I'm going to do reconnaissance."

She sat up straight. "I'm not—"

"A child. I know you don't like being told what to do. So I'll rephrase it. Please sit in the truck while I look around. In fact, scoot on over into the driver's seat and stay low. If you see something suspicious then get out of here. Just drive away."

"I can't just leave you."

He grabbed her hands and held them, like he'd done before. "Yes, you can. You can leave Rich and me. He never wanted you in this to begin with. Think of it this way. If we have to worry about you, then that's a distraction and could get us all killed. For Rich and for me, get out and somewhere safe." At his words, Olivia could almost regret that she'd come at all.

"You're not playing fair, and I know it's not a game." There. She'd cut him off before he could counter. Pulling her hands free, she shifted to stare out her window again, at anything but his persuasive eyes. "You're holding me hostage. If something happens to either of you then I can only blame myself."

"That's not how I meant it."

"Then how did you mean it?" she asked.

"I'm getting out of this truck alone and I'm going to find Rich. When I do, I'll come back and get you. But I don't want to be responsible for putting you in harm's way more than you already are. Now, can you agree to that?"

She nodded. All her arguing wasted valuable time and she knew it. But she hadn't wanted to be left in the truck. Zach opened his door and slid out. She scooted over to the driver's seat.

"Remember. If you see anything suspicious, drive out of here."

Olivia watched him stroll away from her, carrying himself with confidence and like he had not a care in the world except to see if there was room in the inn. He'd been a good-looking guy from the start, but now he'd filled out with those broad shoulders and his sturdy form. She needed to look away from him and watch their surroundings, but her eyes stayed on him until something else caught her attention.

At the far corner of the building, someone stepped from the shadows, the hood of his jacket covering his face, and she decided by his build it was a guy. Had he been hiding? Watching for her and Zach?

She wished both cell phones had charged by now so that she could communicate with Zach to warn him as he entered the lodge. She didn't like that he was out of sight. Then the man, still hunkering behind that hood, followed Zach inside.

So much for sitting in the truck. Olivia climbed out and locked the vehicle, then hurried across the snow-plowed parking lot. Careful to watch her surroundings in case someone had followed them, she also kept an eye out for her brother.

Oh, Rich. Where are you? And what are you doing?

Was he waiting for them at Diamond Lake somewhere else besides the lodge where they'd sometimes stayed to snowmobile when growing up? She served as a snowmobile guide at Diamond Lake for Wilderness, Inc. when customers requested it. Had Rich picked this place because they both knew the trails? She wished she could figure out what he'd been thinking.

Olivia entered the lodge and slowed her pace to allow her eyes to adjust to the lighting. A few people checked in, while others huddled in groups here or there, preparing to head out for their day. An elderly man sat in a plump chair by a massive fire.

But she didn't see Zach.

Nor did she see the man who had entered after him. Her pulse quickened. She tried to act natural as she meandered around the room like she belonged there with the others. A couple of guys looking at their phones glanced up at her and both smiled. Ugh. She looked away. She hadn't come here for that. Plus, she had to look like a wreck.

Zach, where did you go?

Had he gone to use the facilities or was there an exit through the back?

On a hunch, Olivia approached the reservations desk and waited for her turn, considering how she could ask for information about Rich. The woman in front of her was about to finish checking in when an arm wrapped around her waist and ushered her out of line.

"Hey!" She recognized the man's jacket from the shadows and wasn't going to let him rush her away, but he'd whisked her across the lobby and into a side hallway before she recognized him.

"Rich?" She whispered the question.

"It's me, sis."

"You look…different." Haggard.

"I'm tired. And I haven't shaved in a few days."

"Rich, what happened? What's this all about?"

"Not now. Let's get out of here."

"But wait. Zach was with me. Didn't you see him? You walked in right behind him. I didn't recognize you. Couldn't tell it was you beneath the hood, so I thought it was one of the shooters."

Pain etched his features at her words. "Zach went to get you."

"Oh, great. And I'm not going to be there. He'll be upset with me."

"Not when he finds you alive. He'll be happy and will forget he was upset." Rich pushed through the exit in the back. "We're going to take the long way around instead of the front door. We can't be too careful."

Outside he stopped and kept them to the shadows against the wall. His eyes narrowed as though that could help him see better as he searched their surroundings. "Okay, we're good to go."

Even after everything she'd been through the last two days, she hadn't grasped how serious this was until this moment, in her brother's presence. His rigid stance.

Nothing could ever scare him.

And yet her brother looked terrified.

"Let's get out of here. We'll talk later."

At the front corner of the building they stopped. From here, Olivia could watch Zach approach his truck.

"But Zach…he'll think something's happened to me."

"Something *has* happened. To all of us."

"I don't want him to suffer like that."

She witnessed his sudden misstep and hesitation. He stopped. Shoulders drew back.

"Rich, please, I need to tell him. Why are we staying here?"

"He'll live, Olivia. And that's the point. For us to get out of this alive."

Zach continued on to his truck and tried the door but found it locked.

"I have the keys," she whispered.

"That's fine. He'll figure it out."

"What was the plan, Rich?"

"He was going to bring you back inside. You guys need snowmobiles to get to the cabin where I'm staying."

Stumbling, Rich groaned and leaned against the wall.

"Rich!" She kept her voice low and urgent. "Are you all right?"

He'd broken out in a sweat. "No. I need to get back to the cabin. Been waiting here since I got here. Waiting for you and Zach to show. I couldn't know what happened. If you had lived or died. Or if you even found my clue, but I kept thinking if you tried to find me, you would think of the cave where we played. That if injured I would hide there. That's exactly what I did. After I wrecked that snowmobile, I crawled down the creek bed and focused on that cave while I put pressure on my wound. I got to that cave, and while I sat there catching my breath, wrapping the wound with my undershirt, I came up with that crazy idea to leave you a clue just in case we didn't find each other in all this. I knew I had to get out of the area to lead those guys away and then lose them. And if you went to the cave, I could hope you'd see what I'd carved in the wall right next to our other drawings."

He drew in a ragged breath, then said, "When I made it back to Gideon, I searched for you there, too, just in case I could find you, until I saw someone, one of the men I'd worked with. He was there in Gideon, waiting and watching. I knew I couldn't hang around and wait or go back to the house and search for you. So I came here and waited. I didn't know what I was going to do if you didn't show up here today. I knew you should have found it by now."

He slowly slid down the wall. "I guess… I guess now that you're here, the adrenaline keeping me going is crashing."

Strong arms reached down and hefted Rich back to his feet. "I've got you, buddy."

Zach!

Olivia had never been so glad to see him. At that moment, watching him hold her brother up, warmth flooded her heart to overflowing. She wished she hadn't resolved never to love again.

What she didn't know, had yet to figure out, was whether the pain of being alone and watching love pass her by would be less than the pain of a broken heart. Was it worth the risk?

Zach gripped Rich, throwing his arm under Rich's shoulder and around the man's back as he assisted Rich into the cabin not two miles from Diamond Lake in Umpqua National Forest. Ushering his friend over to the couch and settling him there, Zach was surprised Rich had been able to drive his snowmobile and lead them into the woods.

Rich lolled his head back. "Just give me a minute."

Concern spilled from Olivia's eyes as she knelt next to him and unzipped his coat. Her gasp and quick glance at Zach told him enough. He peered closer.

Blood.

"It's nothing." Rich's lids fluttered then his eyes finally opened.

"Nothing? You're bleeding. Is this the wound you incurred back at the house?"

He nodded. "Got some supplies. I did what I could with what I had."

"You mean you stitched it up yourself."

"Yes. I'll live. Took some antibiotics, too. Stop worrying about me. The stupid wound broke open, that's all."

Zach frowned. There was much more going on here. Maybe Rich didn't want to admit it in front of Olivia. As it was, Zach was truly surprised they had found Rich at all. The clue he'd left was flimsy at best, but between the siblings, they'd managed to communicate effectively. Sad they'd been that close growing up and knew each other that well, yet let three years go by without talking. No wonder Olivia carried so much guilt.

"I'll get you some water." Olivia rose from where she knelt, a somber look on her face. She headed to the kitchen.

Zach didn't mean to be insensitive or heartless, but it was time for some answers. "Let us know what we can do to make you more comfortable. Like…take you to a hospital."

"No!" Rich shifted forward, then thought better of it. "I need to rest and I'll be okay."

A slow anger started churning in Zach's gut. Did Rich even get how much danger he'd put his sister in? Zach pulled a chair closer and leaned in. "You contacted me asking me to meet you. You were cryptic in your message. I did what you asked. I'm guessing you were as surprised to see Olivia at the house as I was to find her in the woods looking for you."

His eyes, almost the same as Olivia's except darker, studied Zach. "I didn't mean to involve her. Didn't want to involve you but I had no one else. You're a detective. You can help me with this."

Zach could wait to break the news. He had a feeling even if he'd remained on the Portland PD, this was out of his jurisdiction, and Rich knew that, too. "Help you with what, Rich? I need to know what's going on."

Olivia returned with the water and helped Rich drink it. She'd always been a nurturer and that's why she'd made a great biology teacher. Children, plants or animals, living things thrived in her care, and Rich would too if they lived through this. Zach realized, too, that her attention had shifted away from Zach and onto Rich where it should be. But a cold loneliness filled the space.

"It's a cover-up. It's all about keeping something gone horribly wrong under wraps. I was working, just doing my job on a security detail at a facility in Iraq. We don't ask questions. We're just there to keep the peace, keep people safe. Except everything went wrong."

Rich drank more water. "There's food, a little food in the kitchen, if you're hungry." He forced a smile then coughed from the effort.

"What went wrong, Rich." Zach urged Rich back on topic.

"Someone took a shot. Got nervous, or suspicious, when a car approached. I don't know but the next thing that happened everyone was shooting. And when the dust settled innocent women and children were among the slaughtered. Our next instructions were to cover it all up. News of what happened couldn't get out because we would all pay the price, including someone who invested in the company—some VIP in Washington."

He swiped a hand over his mouth. "I wanted out. I couldn't go along with any of it. But I knew there was no way they could afford to let me go. But they knew…they knew I wasn't okay with what they were doing. I figured it was a matter of time before I was killed in the line of duty. Friendly fire. One night I snuck into an office along with another guy. I lifted information off a computer. Incriminating information—the security video of the entire incident. I got that before they destroyed it, but the owner wanted to view the details to ascertain what had gone wrong and make sure it didn't happen again. In essence I have a whole group of ex-military-grade security people after me. I didn't realize they would go to these lengths to find me. Do you understand now?"

Zach was trying. "So you're in big trouble. Why'd you do it then, Rich? Why did you leave and take information with you? If you'd disappeared without stealing the evidence, maybe there was a chance they might have decided you weren't worth the trouble. But now…"

"No. They would have come after me, regardless. I hadn't counted on them being able to find me so fast. I took it because I thought I might need the leverage to keep me safe, but more than that I wanted to do something right in the world. I wanted to make a difference. Who was I but just some guy out of the military who'd failed his family? But this time, at least I could show the world what had happened."

Tears slid from the corners of Rich's eyes. "And Sarah.

After what happened to Sarah. Oh, man." He scraped a hand over his face to wipe away the evidence. "I should have come home, Olivia. I should have come home for Mom. At least for a while."

Olivia pressed her head into Rich's chest, her shoulders shaking.

Hanging his head, Zach steeled himself against the moment. Against the onslaught of emotion. His failure had caused a landslide as massive as what he'd seen on Mount Thielsen. But none of it mattered at the moment.

"I don't blame you, Zach. I never did."

Zach lifted his face to find Rich looking at him, his features composed.

Emotion bubbled up inside Zach like lava gurgling inside a volcano. He had to gain control of his reaction. "Good to know."

"And Olivia, oh, Olivia, I never meant to involve you. And now you're in trouble because of me. Please forgive me, baby sis."

"It's okay, Rich."

"She was in the wrong place at the wrong time, Rich. That's all," Zach said.

"Please, don't go back to the house on the mountain until this is over and done, you hear me?"

She nodded. "I don't think I was in the wrong place at the wrong time. Just the opposite. I think I was in the right place at the right time. I missed you, Rich, missed you so much. And now that you're back, I'm not about to leave you. We're in this together."

Not exactly what Zach wanted to hear.

Just like Olivia, believing she could fix all that was broken. Well, she hadn't thought Zach was worth it or she would have tried to fix what had gone wrong with them. He pushed away the bitter thought and reminded himself he'd been the one to give *her* up.

What's past is past. Listening to the distant whir of snowmobiles, he focused on the present. He wanted Olivia far away from this and safe. But where in the world any of them could run from this, he didn't know. They would have to see this through and finish it if they wanted their lives back.

He moved them back on point. "Can I ask what happened to the other guy?"

"Jonathan? We split up. Headed in opposite directions. I know he got out of the country."

"You haven't heard from him since?" Olivia asked.

Rich shook his head. "We thought it best if we made no contact. But since they found us at the house, I have to wonder if they got him. We were close. I told him things nobody else knew, before any of this happened. But they could have forced information out of him."

Great. Had Rich told Jonathan about Diamond Lake? He didn't believe his friend was thinking clearly, but he was only human and under a great deal of duress and suffering from a serious gunshot wound, as it was.

Sitting forward, Rich finished the water and set the glass on the table next to the sofa. He put his elbows on his thighs. The guy made an effort to show himself strong, but he needed medical attention. More than that, Zach wasn't sure what Rich expected of them, now that they were here.

"What did you do with the information? I take it you saved it on a thumb drive," Zach said.

"Yes. I hid it somewhere they can't get to it. If something happens to me, at least you could get it and take it to the authorities. There has to be someone you know that you believe will do the right thing with this. I had no one else I could trust to see it through. It's just too indicting. Too big and dangerous."

Zach understood. He could imagine how this would go down. Rich would give the information to the FBI or some other law enforcement entity. The company, the VIP looking for him, could easily shut it down and get their information back and take Rich out, from the sounds of it. Rich had become a whistle-blower in a deadly scenario. His life, all their lives, were forfeit.

Zach needed a glass of water too and moved to the kitchen counter facing south at the front of the one-room cabin. He hovered at the sink longer than necessary to get the water, giving himself time to think. To compose what he would say next. Releasing a long breath, Zach finally told him. "I'm not in law enforcement anymore. I resigned." Though it made no difference either way.

He turned.

A bullet cracked the kitchen window.

THIRTEEN

Terror blasted through Olivia with the clink of the glass window as it spidered.

Zach ducked from the window. Rich rose to his feet as Zach rushed toward them.

"Get down." Zach pushed Olivia to the floor.

"No. We have to get out of here or we'll be trapped." Careful to avoid the windows, Rich crept to the back door. "Come on!"

Nodding his agreement, Zach urged Olivia forward ahead of him and behind Rich. How would they ever get out of this? How would they ever get their lives back?

Rich grabbed three packs, and handed off two. "I prepared for the worst-case scenario. Surviving in the wilderness."

Oh, great. Maybe she was working for Wilderness, Inc. as a guide but she didn't want to actually have to *survive* in the wilderness with killers after them. Rich eased the back door open. They'd parked the snowmobiles behind the cabin that had nearly been buried in snow. And right now, she was glad for the deep snow that would cover them for their escape. But how had they been discovered?

Zach held her back from following Rich out the door. "I'll go next to make sure it's okay, but stay close."

"I don't need you to protect me."

"I know." His gaze pinned her where she stood. "But I need this. Maybe I'm being selfish, but I *need* to protect you, so let me."

He *needed* to protect her?

Oh, please, don't do this, Zach. Don't make me fall for you again.

Funny that Zach was the one to act as her protector, rather than her brother.

Zach eased through the door, his weapon at the ready, and the pack on his back. She was glad they would be riding and not hiking. What had Rich packed in these things?

When Zach turned and motioned for her to follow, she slid through the door and rushed as quickly as she could, burdened with a snowmobile suit and a heavy pack. The machines were still warm from their earlier ride. But riding them, no matter where they went, would leave tracks, and it was doubtful they could lose the men after them. Unless a snowstorm moved in. But maybe they could get lost in a throng of snowmobile enthusiasts out for an afternoon ride. Considered the "gem of the Cascades," the Diamond Lake area was one of the top snowmobiling areas.

And Olivia did not want to go through another storm.

What was Rich's plan? How did he think they could lose the men? Did he even have a strategy? He'd gone to great lengths to keep his whereabouts under wraps. And he'd prepared the backpacks, so he had been thinking ahead. All these thoughts bombarded her as she ran for the snowmobile. Adrenaline threaded through her panic, bringing her back on focus—they had to get away from the cabin.

Standing next to the snowmobiles, they tugged on their helmets and climbed on.

She rested her gloved hand on the handlebars, but waited for Rich to start his vehicle. The motors' roars to life would alert whoever was after them to the fact they were fleeing the cabin. They would need to make a quick escape into the Mount Thielsen Wilderness area, or wherever Rich would lead them.

With a nod, her brother started the ignition. Zach and Olivia did the same. She heard the now more than familiar and unwelcome sound of gunfire.

Oh, no... *God, please, please. I can't take this anymore. Just let it be over.*

Rich turned the vehicle away from the cabin and took off. Olivia glanced at Zach. Would he go next?

He gestured for her to go so he would be last. Speeding up, she fell in behind Rich, frosted-white evergreens whizzing past her on either side of the trail. Following Rich on the snowmobile brought back so many memories of the times they'd spent here when they were young. Hundreds of miles of groomed snowmobile trails waited to be explored, but if she had to guess, Rich would be taking them to some backcountry, ungroomed wilderness trails for advanced riders. Zach could handle them, but she didn't know about the experience levels of the men after them.

It was worth a try.

One of the dangers came when the rolling hills swiftly changed to sharp ridges as they crested toward the Cascade mountain range. As if her thoughts had morphed into reality, Rich took a hard right in front of them to avoid just such a ridge, and went off trail.

She was literally on a ride for her life. And this ride included those she loved.

Loved? She glanced back to Zach in his black suit and helmet with a visor that obscured his face, his intense blue eyes. Turning her focus back to maneuvering over white powder to keep up with Rich, snow splattered her visor and startled her. She wiped it away.

The truth hit her in the face the same way.

She'd never truly stopped loving Zach, just pushed it all into a compartment in her heart. That compartment was threatening to break open now. But she couldn't love him again. Not like before. She swallowed the sudden tears in her throat.

Oh, not now, not now. She couldn't deal with this now when their lives were on the line.

But she failed at pushing the thoughts aside. She was on the verge of losing everything and everyone she cared about in this world. Again!

How could this happen?

Ahead of her, Rich slipped off his snowmobile directly in her path.

Olivia's scream pierced through his helmet.

The horrific scene unfolded before him in slow motion.

She swerved to the right, barely missing Rich's unmoving form splayed in the snow. Momentum fueled Rich's riderless snowmobile forward until it slammed into a tree. At the same moment, Olivia's snowmobile angled over a slope. Only it wasn't riderless.

Fear corded through Zach. She was an experienced rider, but focus was key. The machine tipped.

Lean toward the incline. Lean, lean, lean...

But she didn't lean, her mind obviously still grappling with what had become of Rich.

"No! Olivia!" Zach's booming cry reverberated inside his helmet, stabbing through him. Squeezing the brake lever, he brought his machine to a stop, then hopped off and ran, his booted feet sluggish in layers of white.

Just before her snowmobile rolled, Olivia leapt out of its path. The force of its movement kept it rolling down the slope until the trees caught it. Zach struggled to catch his breath.

Olivia hiked through the waist-deep snow up the slope.

She's okay. She's okay.

His focus shifted.

Rich...

In his helmet, her brother lay facedown in the snow.

Hurtling across the beaten path to his best friend, Zach dropped to his knees, sliding the last few inches toward Rich like he was home base, and beat Olivia to her brother.

Maybe he could protect her, prepare her for the worst.

"Rich!" He lifted the man's head. Rich's face shield was cracked, so Zach rolled him to his back and removed his helmet completely. "Rich..."

His features twisted in pain. "What? I'm okay. I'm good..." He edged up onto his elbows. "What happened?"

Zach allowed relief to roll through him that Rich was still alive. But this new development was not good.

"Apparently you blacked out." And not for just a few seconds.

Olivia had topped the slope. Her face shield up, her pensive gaze sought Zach's.

"Are you able to sit up?" Zach asked Rich, his eyes still on Olivia.

"Sure. I'm okay."

"You keep saying that but I think we need to find you a doctor."

Rich maneuvered onto his haunches and caught Olivia when she almost plowed into him. Somehow she slowed her impetus and instead gently pressed against him, hugging him to her. "Rich, I thought…"

"It's okay, sis. I blacked out. That's all."

She released him and pressed her gloved hands on his cheeks. "You scared me half to death."

"I'm sorry."

Her face scrunched up. "We need to get you to a hospital."

"Right. So I can die at the hands of these killers."

"It's a risk, maybe, but if you need help then we have no choice."

"That's not the only problem we have." Zach got to his feet. He could hear the snowmobiles growing closer. Were their pursuers closing in or was it just enthusiasts? They might have lost their pursuers, but only temporarily. Zach eyed Rich's snowmobile crushed against the tree. A complete loss.

"I'm going to check on the machine at the bottom of the slope. See if I can right it and bring it back up. We're down to two machines now." Fortunately, each of them could accommodate more than one person, or they'd all be on foot.

Rich didn't appear to be in any condition to hike. That was troubling, considering they would have to travel a long way to escape with their lives. As cold seeped into Zach's bones and hunger gnawed in his gut, he thought maybe the ends of the earth might not be far enough.

Zach left them and headed off to see if he could retrieve Olivia's snowmobile. That machine could be damaged beyond repair, too, which sent his thoughts to Rich. Before his friend succumbed to his injuries, Zach needed to find out more. Rich still hadn't told him what he'd done with the thumb drive. Why was he holding back?

Finding the path in the snow that Olivia's snowmobile had created on the way down, Zach used it, but the effort of pushing through the waist-high layers remained and battered his already exhausted body. Despite finding Rich, they hadn't escaped this terrible ordeal. They had only traded one wilderness for another, and still killers pursued them.

One thing at a time. One problem at a time, though they were beginning to add up exponentially.

From a distance, Zach studied the snowmobile as he made his way down.

He could see the machine against a tree. How hard had it hit? That's what mattered most. Likely the roll down the hill on the soft snow would have slowed it enough to soften the impact.

Maybe nothing vital had been damaged. He could only hope. And pray. Pain lanced his heart. If he thought about it too hard, he had to admit he felt bruised. Emotionally and psychologically—his life had been like a rushing, wild, abusive river, dashing him against the rocks, spearing him with debris. His soul ached so much that his pain had become physical.

God, nothing in my life has turned out like I thought. Like I have hoped and prayed. Nothing. What is with

You, God? Why do we have to work to live, fight to survive? Do You want these guys to kill us or what? Why can't we catch a break?

Zach didn't like where his prayer had gone, but he couldn't stop the silent words flowing from his heart now that he'd opened that door. But he figured if it was in his heart God already knew it. No point in lying about it. Maybe Zach was the one who needed to know what was in his heart. Maybe these fiery trials of the last few years had forced all the bad inside him to float to the top so he could see it. But seeing it there, and acknowledging all his anger toward God, didn't help him one iota when it came to their current predicament.

He made it to the snowmobile and found the skis up against the tree. Didn't like what he saw. Glancing back up the slope, he checked to see if anyone watched. No one stood there to witness what would happen next. Their hopes of escaping were wrapped up in this one machine.

"We need a break, God. We need some help here."

He positioned himself to push the machine from the tree. Groaning with the strain of every muscle, he pushed it off the trunk, scraping more bark away. It plopped forward and onto the snow. A few pants and he'd caught his breath. Zach walked around the length of it. Would it run? Only one way to find out.

He climbed on, started the ignition, grateful to hear the noise, and hit the throttle.

Thanks, God.

If he was going to ask for something and his prayer was answered, he'd better remember to give thanks.

His weight to the rear of the snowmobile, he leaned forward to a kneeling position, increasing traction in the front, and then he accelerated up the hill. On the slope's ascent, he throttled it, increasing as necessary so he could maintain speed and momentum. If he rolled this thing again they could forget about it.

Though their predicament was far from over, Zach let the hope of this moment bolster his confidence and he made it to the top. Steering the machine closer to Olivia and Rich, who remained sitting, he expected a smile or a cheer. But that's not what he got.

He climbed off. "We're back in business."

Olivia had removed her helmet and her brown, coppery mane contrasted with the frosted pines behind her. The image could have sucked his breath away except for the worry in her eyes. That alone crippled him.

"What is it?" He stumbled forward and fought the need to catch her up in his arms as she rushed to meet him.

"I know why Rich fell off. He has another gunshot wound. It must have happened when we escaped from the cabin. I don't... I don't know if he's going to make it."

FOURTEEN

The threat of losing her brother again, and this time forever, stared her down—looming in her near future. That is, if she didn't do something about it. But what could they do? Rich had led them out into the middle of nowhere with limited communication, though he'd packed a SAT phone and she had the one cell that had charged. Their goals had been reduced to the simple matter of survival.

Survive the moment.

Survive the day.

He'd done the only thing he could do.

"We have to do something!" she cried out. Her brother held it together for her. Acting strong, burning through his reserves. For her and Zach. But he couldn't keep this up. He couldn't last much longer like this. "Zach, do you hear me? We can't keep going like this."

"You're wrong. *We* can."

The way he said *we* filled her with dread. "What are you saying? That we're just going to leave him behind? We have to help him."

Zach pushed by her and went to Rich. "Show me."

Wrapping his arms around himself, Rich averted his

bloodshot gaze. "I've got it." He squeezed tighter, unwilling to reveal the damage. "We don't have time. They're coming. You lost *your* sister—the woman who would have been my wife. Now is your chance to do things right. Are you going to save my sister or not?" Glaring at Zach, Rich ground out the words. "Get her out of here!"

Zach's features morphed, changing him into someone she barely recognized.

Oh, no. God, please no. "Zach. He didn't mean it. He's out of his head. We're not leaving him."

Rich continued to argue. To her relief, Zach assisted him to his feet, and wrapped an arm under Rich's shoulder and around his back, then, together, they hobbled over to Zach's snowmobile.

"You'll ride with me. You can't drive anyway. Just as well since we only have two left."

Rich struggled to get on, huffing and grunting as he positioned himself against the backrest supported by the luggage rack holding Zach's pack. Zach retrieved Rich's pack from his snowmobile and secured it on top of that. But Rich appeared to have lost the strength to do anything except follow directions, if that.

Nausea rolled through Olivia. At least when they were in the Siskiyou Mountains, and she wasn't sure if he was alive or dead, she could hope he was alive and well. But now, seeing him like this, their life-and-death predicament rocked through her.

Zach dug in his pack and pulled out a rope. "I'll strap you to me just in case you pass out again." His gaze flicked to Olivia's. "We don't want to risk losing you."

She was grateful, so grateful for Zach. While she wouldn't want to wish this on anyone, if she had to have anyone else with her, helping her to fight and win, that person was Zach.

Olivia got on the snowmobile Zach had retrieved for her. In the distance, she could hear other snowmobiles drawing closer. Was it riders out for a good time? Or those searching for them? Had they brought danger to innocent people? But where could they have fled except to the wilderness to lessen collateral damage?

After securing Rich to him as he sat on the two-seater, Zach pulled on his helmet. He lifted the visor and caught her attention. "You know the region. You lead us out."

"Where are we going? Where should I lead us?" The network of trails could take them all the way to Bend or even Klamath Falls.

"Anywhere but here."

She could do that. They had to escape. Rich needed medical attention and soon. She wouldn't take him back to Diamond Lake where the threat of danger could still be waiting on them.

Olivia nodded, flipped down her visor. She would lead them back to the groomed trail between Diamond Lake and Crater Lake. That would take a good forty-five minutes and get them to the north entrance of Crater Lake. She'd led a few guided tours there. She knew where to find a ranger station. It was all she could think of. Park rangers were trained to assist in medical emergencies, and would have the necessary supplies and abilities to save Rich.

Gunning the engine, she zoomed forward across the snow-globe landscape, and hoped they didn't run into the men after them.

God, please let him live. Please let him live until we

can find him help. And while You're at it, keep us safe. Help us to find the right law enforcement entity to bring justice.

Glancing over her shoulder, she made sure that Zach remained behind her. The sun broke through the gray blanket for a few moments and allowed her to see the mountains and jagged cliffs, but soon ducked behind the clouds again. Snowflakes hit her visor. A headwind slowed her push forward, and drove the snowflakes horizontal. She groaned at the thought of another storm, but maybe they could push through it. Approaching nine thousand feet elevation, she had to expect inclement weather to show up without warning.

The main problem was visibility. She needed to see the trail, and she needed to find that ranger station. All around them, the scenery had turned into nothing but a white abyss. She couldn't see ten feet in front of her, and the trail quickly disappeared.

They pushed through into a wide-open space of what used to be groomed trails, and she spotted the top of the sign that marked Crater Lake National Park and kept going.

And searching.

Steering the snowmobile in this weather made searching for the ranger station a difficult task. A few more miles and Olivia slowed the machine to a stop, and waited for Zach to pull up next to her. She glanced at Rich, who gave her a thumbs-up. She didn't believe him. Zach lifted his visor. "Problem?"

The low visibility had driven her too far and she'd passed the ranger station she'd been searching for. "I'm not sure where I am."

"Are you telling me we're lost?"

* * *

"We want to get lost," Rich said. "We want to be far away from anyone who can hurt us." Rich slurred his words and sounded drunk.

"We're not lost. We can't get lost on the trails. Eventually we'll get there." Olivia had flipped up her visor and searched in both directions.

Eventually? They didn't have that kind of time. Rich was fading.

Zach hated where his thoughts took him but was surprised the guy was still with them. Either alive or conscious. They wanted to lose their pursuers, yes, but they needed a game plan. Shelter, water and food, in that order. And to connect with someone with authority who could take this burden from them. He wasn't sure what he'd expected once they had found Rich. His only thought had been to find his friend in the first place. Their pursuers had tracked them again. How?

"Where are you trying to take us, Olivia?"

"We're turning around. I'm looking for the ranger station, where we can get Rich help."

Zach nodded.

"No…no, no…" Rich groaned behind him.

"We have no choice, buddy," Zach said.

Fearing for all their lives, Rich hadn't wanted them to make contact with any authorities until they zeroed in on someone who could be trusted to see this through. But under the circumstances, that was the least of Rich's worries.

A ranger station wasn't the hospital, but the ranger might know where the nearest clinic would be, or would have the supplies and could assist in either getting or giving emergency medical assistance.

Rich tried to get off the snowmobile, pulling against

the rope that bound them. Zach ground his teeth. Pulled free and climbed off the machine. He grabbed Rich's shoulders. His eyes were shut and pain lined his face as he lolled to the side. Uh-oh.

Zach shot a glance at Olivia. She watched in a daze, a stricken look on her face.

Suddenly, her features morphed into horror. "Behind you! Look out!"

He turned as a bullet grazed his shoulder for the second time in two days. Rich fell completely off the snowmobile. Zach scrambled around behind the machine to see to Rich. At least he'd fallen in the right direction.

How many times would Zach be stuck behind a snowmobile, hiding from shooters?

"You okay?" he called out to Olivia.

She fired off shots from behind her snowmobile with the weapon Rich had given her. That answered his question. Time for them to move. If they tried to climb onto the machines, they would be too exposed. Better make for the trees.

Olivia shot a few more rounds and Zach lifted Rich and dragged him off the groomed trail to the cover of trees. He situated Rich against a trunk, then he fired his weapon at the shooters and Olivia crawled over to the trees.

"How many are there, did you see?"

"Just one that I could see." She caught her breath, then looked at her brother. "Rich?"

Olivia grabbed his face and stared into it. "Rich!"

Her brother was unresponsive. Zach checked his pulse. He was still with them.

"What are we going to do, Zach? This situation is impossible. It's like God has forgotten us."

"Right now, we're in survival mode. Nothing more

important than getting away from that shooter. I think we're going to have to take this to someone else or find ourselves constantly on the run."

"What about Rich?"

"Let's get him out of here."

"How are we going to do that without getting shot? We've been through this before. The guy shot his own partner. They are focusing on killing Rich."

"And are close to succeeding."

She sucked in a breath. "Zach…you've been shot."

She examined his sliced shoulder sleeve, her eyes slowly pulling up to meet his. "You're bleeding."

Her form deflated and her face paled.

He pulled her to him then. "It's only a graze. I'm not going to die. Not yet. Listen, Olivia, I need you to hold it together."

She stiffened at that. Sat taller. "What are you talking about? I'm not holding it together enough for you?"

Good girl. He knew he would get a rise out of her. That's what he'd been aiming for. "You're doing great."

With everything that had gone wrong to pull them apart and keep them apart, he never could have imagined they would be thrown together again in a game of survival.

He tucked his fears and regrets, all his emotions away for now. "I need you to stay here."

Zach started forward.

Olivia grabbed him. "Wait, where are you going?"

"Stay here with your brother, Olivia. I'm going to get rid of this guy." Sure. Like it would be that easy. "And if Rich wakes up, find out where he hid the information."

He left her and Rich alone.

God, please keep them safe. I can't have their lives on

my hands, as well. Protect us from these people. Make a path for us.

Behind a thick group of pines, Zach waited and listened. He watched Olivia and Rich. He saw nothing. Heard nothing. Where had the shooter gone?

He made his way from tree to tree and then to the snowmobiles, hoping no other snowmobilers came upon them, unwittingly putting themselves in danger. He eyed the trees across the trail where the shots had come from. The low visibility wasn't working in his favor.

Zach fired his weapon at them. He got no shots in return.

It was a risk, but one he'd have to take. He sucked in two quick breaths, then ran the rest of the way across the wide groomed trail. Climbed over the snow berm created from grooming. On the other side, Zach held his weapon up and plopped in the snow while he caught this breath. His pulse soared too high.

Nothing. Had the guy crossed the trail already?

But then he spotted him.

Splayed out in the snow in a pool of blood.

One of their shots had caught him. Zach plowed through the deep snow to the man, checked his pulse and found none. Unfortunately, he spotted tracks leading away. There was another shooter. Zach could follow them, but for how long? A sense of urgency that he needed to get back to Olivia and Rich descended on him. He crossed the trail again and followed his path through the trees, watching for the other shooter.

He hiked through the snow to where he'd left Olivia and Rich.

They were gone.

FIFTEEN

Breathe, just breathe. Olivia panted with each step as she plowed through the snow, limbs growing numb, muscles straining against Rich's weight.

"Come on, you can do it." Olivia half dragged her semiconscious brother.

A man—one of the shooters—hiked through the woods, searching for them. She'd seen him in the distance, barely glimpsing him through the heavy snowfall.

Had the man killed Zach?

Oh, God, please...no. Her heart couldn't take the possibility. Her mind wouldn't accept it. But he'd gone to take this man down. Or had there been more than one? Regardless, she was out of ammo and only had a knife left with which to fight. He would find them. All he had to do was follow their trail through the snow to this tree. Though it seemed a blizzard had descended on them, it wouldn't cover their tracks fast enough.

Nothing left to do but run.

As she'd assisted Rich to his feet and they went deeper into the forest away from the trail, she'd seen the ranger station in the distance. There was no time to lose.

Rich was fading fast.

A killer was coming after them.

And Olivia was running out of time.

One of those gunshots in their most recent firefight had gotten him. She hadn't discovered it until Zach had already gone. Olivia had never met a stronger person than her brother. Rich had the will to live and that was key. But she had to get him help. Zach could fend for himself. When he came back for them he could follow their footprints in the snow or he'd see the backside of the ranger station in the distance just as she had. But she couldn't wait for him. The station should be staffed and if it was a visitor center, too, she hoped she wasn't bringing trouble to others.

"Just a little farther." Nearly breathless, Olivia wasn't sure if she was reassuring herself or Rich.

With each breath, each step, she could feel the killer closing in. She risked a glance behind her. There. He was a hundred yards back. Faster. They had to move faster.

"Come on, Rich! We have to get inside."

He groaned with the effort.

"We're going to die if we don't get away."

Zach, where are you? God, where are You?

Her muscles screamed, refusing to move faster or work harder.

Come on, come on, come on...

Together, they limped toward the ranger station, the snow impeding their efforts.

A figure emerged from the door at the back and rushed to her aid, taking her place. A park ranger.

Thank You, God!

"He's been shot. He needs emergency medical treatment." Olivia turned to face the killer, walking backward. "There's a man trying to kill us."

But the man had disappeared.

Olivia's chest rose and fell as she caught her breath. They'd made it! And the killer hadn't been willing to pursue them into the public area and ranger station where the park rangers—the law enforcement of the forest—could protect her.

Grimacing, the ranger ushered Rich through the front door of the small substation and into a back room. Laid him on a table.

Olivia followed him. "He needs a doctor or he's not going to make it."

"Not to worry. As an NPS park ranger I'm certified as a wilderness first responder and medical technician, though I'll have to say I haven't treated a gunshot victim, especially one with multiple wounds. I didn't hear any gunfire, but the storm likely muted the sound." The ranger had removed Rich's shirt and hooked him up to an IV. Now he glanced up at her, his gaze hard. "Tell me what happened."

Olivia didn't know what to say. She'd known this moment would come, but they'd tried so hard to keep it a secret. "There are men trying to kill my brother, and now me and my friend, who is still out there somewhere. I'm worried that he's hurt, too. Can you help me? Help us?"

"The men who shot your brother? Are they still out there?"

"Yes. One man was following us but I made it to the station before he could get to us. He might still try something. You could be in danger."

"I'll call for assistance as soon as I get his bleeding under control. I need to save your brother, if I can. You're fortunate you arrived when you did. I just got here myself. I was about to close up until the blizzard passes. Not that anyone is out on the roads in this weather." He eyed her, an apology in his gaze. "I'll at least try to get him stable for the trip to a medical facility. But you might want to say a prayer."

She decided the ranger had kind eyes. "Please, do what you can."

But, God, please don't let this ranger get hurt because I came here to ask for help.

There, she'd said a prayer like he'd suggested. "So you're here alone, then?"

"Yes. For the moment."

Not good. So not good.

Olivia let him focus on giving Rich his full attention and she watched the windows and the doors. These men had tried to kill all three of them, focusing their efforts on Rich this time. But if they killed Rich, how would they get the thumb drive back, or did they even know about it or care? But they had to care. That information in the wrong hands could do them damage, considering the kind of effort they'd put into keeping it quiet.

A bell sounded as the door opened in the front room.

Olivia stiffened and shared a look with the ranger. He stood tall, his gloved hands covered in blood. He ripped off the gloves and grabbed his weapon. Good. He was taking her seriously.

"Get behind me."

She did as he said, and then he crept over and peeked out.

"Olivia?"

"Zach!" She rushed past the ranger and into his arms. "You made it. I was so afraid you were hurt."

He pulled his helmet off, and tugged her closer. He

sank his face into her neck. "I thought I'd lost you." Emotions choked his words.

And hearing that nearly undid her. What was happening to them?

He released her and held her at arm's length. "What happened? Why did you leave?"

"The shooter. I saw him looking for us. Didn't you see him?"

"It's snowing so hard out there I could barely find my way. I saw no one. But I caught a glimpse of this cabin and hoped you might be here."

"Rich was shot again." Olivia pressed her face into Zach's chest then. She had to hold it together. "He's dying. I think he's dying."

"Don't talk like that." Zach took the lead and dragged Olivia into the back room where the ranger had successfully stopped the bleeding in Rich's latest gunshot wound.

Frowning, he looked up at Zach. "He's lost a lot of blood." He snapped off the gloves. "Now, to call for help, get the law in here to catch these guys. I'll need you two to stay here."

He gave them a commanding look then exited the room, leaving them alone with Rich.

The injured man lifted a hand. "Zach."

Both Olivia and Zach rushed to his side. "I'm here, buddy."

"Get her out of here! Get her somewhere safe."

"I'm not sure I know where that is, Rich. We have to tell the police. We can't keep this secret anymore."

Rich nodded. "Find someone. You must know someone who can help."

"Sure, but tell me where you hid the drive."

Closing his eyes, he relaxed.

"Is he unconscious again? Or..." *Dead?* She couldn't say the words. But no, she saw his chest rise and fall.

"Come on, Rich, tell me what I need to know." Zach's tone held no compassion for his seriously injured friend.

But Olivia understood his frustration. Her brother's lashes fluttered then his lids opened, revealing bloodshot eyes that looked at Olivia as he spoke. "I'll tell you, I promise. But you have to promise me that once I do, you will take Olivia and leave. Get as far away from here as you can. Leave Oregon. Leave the country. Whatever it takes until you're safe."

Rich asked a lot. Olivia didn't think Zach would be able to promise that. Who said she wanted that much protection anyway? Who said she wanted to spend that much time with Zach?

"Promise me!"

Standing near her, Zach cleared his throat. His gaze slid to Olivia—and she saw that he was torn inside, just as she was. "I promise."

Rich nodded, releasing a gargled breath. "I hid it in a locker at the snowmobile rentals in Gideon."

"What?" Both Olivia and Zach asked.

But Rich didn't answer. He was out of it. Olivia grabbed Rich's hand, grateful the ranger station was prepared to deal with a medical emergency—and that made sense. This far away from services, they'd need something in case one of the many tourists got injured. But she wasn't sure it was going to be enough.

Pressing herself forward against his hand, she tried to hold back the sobs. Always holding them back. But why? No. She'd let the tears come, and the sobs wrack her body while Rich was still alive. She couldn't lose him, too. Not like this. How she regretted the years they weren't in contact. Not even a phone call.

Olivia wasn't sure how long she stayed that way, but she became aware that Zach had left the room. To give her privacy? She appreciated him. But he'd made a promise he couldn't keep. They both knew that.

Torn about what to do, Zach left Olivia with her brother. Seeing her like that twisted him into knots, turned him inside out. Left him raw. He was a coward to leave her there.

No. Giving her privacy was the right thing to do.

He closed the door behind him and heard the click as the latch engaged. Besides, he was on a mission.

He found the ranger at his radio, making all the necessary calls for help. Glancing through the small lobby and visitor center, Zach confirmed they were alone. The inclement weather had likely sent snowmobilers home or for cover. So far, no one had shown up here. That was fortunate for them. There was no way of knowing what would happen next. If their pursuers would burst through the doors and gun them all down. A little healthy fear rolled over him.

The ranger ended a round of calls. Hands on his hips, he stared at Zach. "Let's hear your side of the story."

"I was hoping you'd say that." Zach could see by the badge the ranger wore that this man was a federal law enforcement officer, a commissioned ranger—he had the full authority of the federal and state laws behind him in this national park. Zach tugged his gun out from where he'd hidden it and rested it on the table between them. "My name is Zachary Long. I used to be in law enforcement. A detective with the Portland PD." Then Zach told him everything.

"That's some story." The ranger eyed him long and hard, then, "I'm Garret Taggart. You any kin to Gifford Long?"

Uh-oh. This could be good. Or this could be bad.

"Yes. He's my father."

Had Ranger Taggart relaxed just a little? Or had Zach imagined it?

"My father worked with yours before he moved to Phoenix. That was years ago. I knew your dad. Met him a couple of times, is all. Good man."

Zach searched his memory. He vaguely recalled the name, but Zach would have been much younger at the time. Asserting himself, taking a chance, he leaned closer. "Then I'm going to ask for a favor here. Olivia's brother asked me to keep her safe. These men want to kill her as well as her brother. I need to get her out of here. Your backup isn't getting here anytime soon, am I right?"

Ranger Taggart leaned back and rubbed his moustache. "The weather will slow them down, but I agree. If everything you've told me is true, and I have no reason to distrust you, then take her away from here. Leave me all your contact information for my investigation. As soon as this blizzard lets up and your friend here is taken care of, I'll hike out to find the body of the shooter and bring that in." He frowned. "Sounds like you've left a trail of blood everywhere you've been. I wouldn't want to be in your shoes."

"You might consider leaving with us. We could somehow secure Rich and take him out of here, too. I'm not so sure you should stay."

The man straightened to well over six feet and sucked

in a breath. “I need to stay and man my post. I have plenty of ammo and others are on the way. There might be a few stranded snowmobilers needing to shelter from the storm even though I’ve officially closed the place. I can’t leave. You take my vehicle and the girl and get her out of here. We’ll be in touch. I’ll do my best by your friend.”

Zach nodded and they worked out the details. Answering a call on his radio, Ranger Taggart dismissed him. Zach headed back to face Olivia. See if she had cried all her tears over Rich. Entering the room, he found her pressing her forehead against Rich’s arm. Gently, Zach urged her up and away from her brother. She didn’t come willingly.

Eyes red and puffy, she hung her head. Tried to look away. Zach lifted her chin to face him. He had a feeling she knew what was coming.

“I have to honor Rich’s request and take you out of here. Get you to safety.”

“No. I’m not leaving him. You can’t keep that promise, and you know it.”

“If nothing else, we need to draw the killers off and away from Rich. You agree with that, don’t you?”

“That’s hardly keeping me safe.”

She was right. His two goals were diametrically opposed. What should he do?

Lord, help me!

He arched a brow. “You’re right. It’s a dangerous fence we’re straddling, but if Rich has any chance of living, we need to draw those guys away from here. And I don’t feel comfortable just sitting here and waiting. So let whatever law enforcement and medical services that descend on this place take over.”

"That ranger isn't going to let us leave. You know that."

"You're wrong."

"What? How?"

"I told him everything. He knows that staying here could be dangerous for us."

"But help is on the way."

"And how long will that take? Besides, he's from Portland. His father used to be with the PD there and knew Dad. That was years before I came and went. I gave him our contact information and he charged me with getting you to safety, just like your brother."

She studied him like she didn't believe him. "Really?"

"Yes. Really."

"And just how are we getting out of here with a storm raging outside? If we have to trek through the woods or ride snowmobiles, we might as well stay here. It would be safer. That's my two cents and I'm sticking to that." Crossing her arms, she rubbed them.

Probably to chase away the chill. Nothing either one of them could do about their exhaustion until this was over.

Zach tossed keys up, then caught them again. "I'm using the vehicle out back. We found what we came for—your brother. We know as much as we need to know and there's nothing more we can do for him, except pray." Had he really said that? "We're heading straight to Gideon to retrieve the thumb drive. I can come back to get my truck later." Driving in this weather would be tricky, but Zach was on a mission. Nobody could stand in his way.

"You mean if someone doesn't kill us first."

What did she want from him? Did she honestly think he could just escape the country with her like Rich suggested and they would live out their lives on some island? "I promised him to keep you safe. Ending this is the only way to do that. Once we hand this off to the right person then and only then will you be safe."

And then Zach might keep his promise and take her somewhere far away from here under completely different circumstances that wouldn't include looking over their shoulders for killers. But he didn't add that in. A thrill rushed through him at the image that came to mind, but his heart was in the wrong place entirely—a place he'd sworn off.

He led her out of the room after she gave Rich one last goodbye though he likely hadn't heard. Zach might have come off hard and cold where Rich was concerned when the guy had sacrificed so much and done the best he could do. But what had they gone through this ordeal for if they all died and the information was lost forever?

No. He had to leave his friend, Olivia's brother, here with Ranger Taggart.

Take care of him, God. Keep him safe. And help me keep Olivia safe.

Still on his radio, the ranger nodded to them as they left. Zach hadn't thought his past career would come to any use in this particular situation—at least not in the way Rich had hoped—but Ranger Taggart had used his discretion and given Zach the chance to get Olivia to safety, probably because of Zach's connection to the Portland PD and the fact Ranger Taggart's father knew Zach's father.

He'd been praying for a break. Maybe this was just the one he needed.

Before they exited the ranger station, Zach eyed the woods. The blizzard would make it hard for help to arrive, whether law enforcement entities, rangers or otherwise, or medical services. And it would also make it difficult for them to leave, but they had to try. They had to use this storm to their advantage.

Inside the vehicle behind the ranger station, Zach started it up and sent up a prayer for the ranger who guarded Rich and, so far, had saved his life. Zach second-guessed his decision to leave the man. To leave Rich. But the magnitude of this situation presented him with no real options.

Once again his life was on a path not of his making—he had no real control over the wild river that swept him away, much like the Rogue River coursing through this part of Oregon. But maybe if he just let go and let the river carry him, instead of trying to fight his way free, he would survive.

But more importantly, Olivia would survive. At that moment, he realized just how important it was that she live through this. He had a feeling that somehow, it would all come down to his life for hers.

And he was willing to pay the price.

SIXTEEN

Sitting in the passenger seat, Olivia held on to the handgrip, her knuckles white. She didn't like driving in a blizzard. A whiteout. But once they got out of the higher elevation of the Cascades, visibility would go up and the driving wouldn't be as hazardous.

But they hadn't run into any more trouble. That disturbed her. Leaving the ranger station near Crater Lake had been too easy. Though she'd hoped and prayed for things to go smoothly, now that they were, tension corded her back. She didn't want to broach a topic that would distract Zach. The guy was entirely too tense, but…

"We're being watched."

"What?" He jerked the steering wheel and they almost fishtailed.

Her heart jumped to her throat.

"Watch it!" Breathe. "Watch the road."

When his lips thinned, she knew he wanted to give her a piece of his mind.

"What do you mean we're being watched? Do you see someone? Be specific, will you?"

"Nothing like that. I just have that feeling you get when someone is watching you."

He kept his focus on the drive along the two-lane curvy road out of Crater Lake. And said nothing at all. Maybe he wasn't taking her seriously.

"Think about it. Someone had to have followed us to find us at that cabin where Rich hid and waited. There could have been a tracking device on your truck. Or maybe you watched for a tail coming out of the Siskiyou Mountains, but you didn't see one." Oh. Now she regretted those words. She could have said them in a different way. Disappointment wasn't what Zach needed to hear from her, and she hadn't meant the words that way at all.

"Whatever. It's all a moot point now," he huffed.

Just as she suspected, he'd taken her words wrong. "Is it? Because if they're still following us, Zach, then we're in big trouble."

And so was Rich. He could already be dead. She hated the morbid thoughts accosting her. But they couldn't let their guards down now. Not until they ended this. She looked out the passenger window at the huge flakes that reduced visibility and forced Zach to drive much too slowly.

He slammed his fist into the dashboard, drawing her head back around.

"What was that for?" she asked.

"Nothing. I don't like any of this. I didn't ask for it. I don't want it." His knuckles turned white as he squeezed the steering wheel.

"Right, like I asked for it."

"I'm not saying you did, or that Rich did. But you think we should have done something differently, don't you?"

Though he'd been the one to ask that question, she could tell that Zach second-guessed himself. Reconsidered his decisions. But it was too late for all of them. The choices had been made.

"Just because I said someone followed us, and I feel like we're being watched, doesn't mean I think you haven't been making good decisions."

And as she said the words, the sun peeked through the clouds—this storm was moody, if anything. Ahead, she could see a clearing in the sky where they'd come out of the mountains. Zach had gone quiet on her again. Just as well. She would keep talking now that she'd opened that floodgate on everything she'd kept dammed up.

Except, suddenly, Zach steered toward the side of the road and put the truck in Park.

He shifted in his seat to look at her. "What about now?"

"Huh?"

"What about now? Do you have that feeling you get when someone is watching you?" His blue gaze turned gray with the weather, pinned her in the seat.

She couldn't move. Couldn't breathe.

Everything else went out of focus and she only saw Zach.

The way he looked at her. Everything inside she'd thought had burned up was like ashes tossed to the wind then rushing together again to form something new. But what? How did she define how he made her feel at this moment? There were no words. And she didn't have the strength to subdue the power he had over her. She swallowed the knot in her throat. "What are you playing at, Zach?"

"Nothing." Pain flashed in his eyes, then he turned his focus back to the road.

He grabbed the shift but she touched his arm, stopping him.

"Wait. Zach..."

He hesitated, then left the truck in Park, but he stared ahead, brooding. She hadn't responded to him in the way she figured he'd expected. But he'd surprised her. Maybe he'd surprised himself. Was that it?

"We need to get going and get this over with," he said.

Get this over with. He couldn't wait to be rid of her. But it didn't matter. She needed to tell him. He needed to know. "My brother called you for help because he knew he could count on you. You're trustworthy and dependable and I just wanted you to know that I believe in you, too. You shouldn't second-guess yourself so much. You told me that if you'd had it to do over again, that you wouldn't have taken the job. Well, if I had it to do over again, I wouldn't have tried to stop you. I would have come with you, if you wanted me to."

Unable to keep watching his profile, the pain in his expression as she spoke, Olivia dropped her gaze and stared at her hands. There. She'd said what she needed to say. But to what purpose, she didn't know.

"Why are you telling me this now?"

"We don't know what's going to happen. Things need to be said, just in case the worst happens. I would regret it if I never told you. Plus, you're too hard on yourself, and I..." It was too painful to watch him beat himself up for every mistake he'd ever made, starting with leaving her, then losing Sarah and now this.

Please don't let me cry again!

She swiped at her eyes. "I'm sorry, Zach. I'm sorry. It's been a long hard day and we're both tired. Can we just get back on the road and get this over with?" To use his own words.

"As you wish." He shifted back into Drive and steered onto the road.

Olivia glanced into the rearview mirror. Was there someone behind them? Not that she could see.

Still, that eerie sensation of being watched settled over her.

Steering back onto the road he could barely see, Zach focused on driving. But he glanced in the rearview mirror. He saw no one behind them. Who would be out driving in this besides someone in a desperate circumstance? Still, he remained wary. When the view became completely white, obscured by thick, wind-driven snow, he opened the truck door.

"What are you doing?" Olivia asked. He didn't miss the fear in her tone.

"I can't see the road any other way." And he stared down and followed the yellow lines as he drove.

This was dangerous beyond words. But it wouldn't be the first time he'd done it. Finally, chunks of asphalt appeared and Zach shut the door. He could see the road again.

He tried to release some of the tension to no avail.

Zach had left his best friend behind. To die, for all he knew. And the thought sickened him. Why didn't life give him a break? Why were his choices never any choice at all?

Choose between the woman you love and the job of your dreams.

Choose between saving your best friend's life and saving the life of his sister, the woman you used *to love.* Yeah, he'd keep that feeling where it needed to stay.

Any way he looked at it, there were no good options.

At least he'd met Ranger Taggart. Zach could trust the ranger. He'd had no choice there either. The decision had been made and now he had this chance, this one chance to see this through and keep Olivia safe. If he could just solve this problem for Rich and end it, Olivia and Rich could have their lives back.

And maybe…just maybe, Zach could have his life back, too.

Maybe he'd have to go through psychological testing and therapy before they'd let him come back to the Portland PD, but so be it. That is, if he ever wanted to go back into law enforcement. Maybe he could be a ranger instead, like Ranger Taggart. Regardless of what his future looked like, he needed this win to fix the past, though he hadn't realized it until that moment. Or maybe he'd still be haunted, anyway, but it was worth a try.

He reached over and grabbed Olivia's hand. Squeezed. She gave him a look. *What are you doing?* He didn't know, but hearing her tell him the words—she would have done it all differently now—had done him a world of good.

It was all in the past, and they could never go back, he knew that, but he was all for going forward. Maybe they could both move forward with their lives with new purpose, free from their past issues. He'd never been so philosophical, but going through a life-and-death crisis did that to you every time. He hoped this would be the last time.

He released her hand, and immediately missed the softness, the connection. He shoved away the regret over losing her.

Finally coming out of the mountains, the snow had

let up, leaving them with an actual road to drive on, and breathtaking scenery.

Leaving him to focus on their next moves. "When we get to Gideon, I'm going to get that thumb drive. You don't need to come with me for that. I'll leave you in the capable hands of Cooper and Gray Wilde, and I'll turn the drive over to the sheriff and let him deal with it."

"No, Zach. You can't do that. What's the sheriff going to do with it? Hand it off to some government agency who will investigate it and possibly shove it in a corner again? Politics, it's always about politics. I won't let you do that."

He popped the steering wheel. "Just what do you think we should do with it then?"

"I have an idea. Cooper's father has big connections. He runs a wilderness training center for all kinds of military groups and government agencies. I hear he has connections with the CIA, even. We can trust him, Zach. Why don't we talk to Cooper and go to him?"

"Why didn't you think of him earlier?"

"I hardly had the chance. Besides, I wanted to find Rich. That was my focus, and we didn't know what my brother was up to anyway. We didn't know about the thumb drive containing evidence."

"Relax. No need to give me excuses. Believe me. I understand. We're both running on adrenaline here."

"So we're good to talk to Cooper about this? See if he can call his father into it?"

"It sounds like the best option to me. All we have to do now is get that thumb drive and stay alive until it's over."

"You don't ask for much, do you?"

Zach stopped for fuel again before they entered the drive into the Wild Rogue Wilderness that would take them to Gideon. And again, Olivia visited the facilities and got them some snacks.

When she returned, she stepped up to him while he fueled his truck. "I want to apologize for that comment I made about you not asking for much, like you aren't capable of seeing this through. You totally are. I made it sound like I didn't believe you could keep us safe and alive. I realize now what you went through before with Sarah, and that you let that eat you up every day until you couldn't work in law enforcement anymore."

He angled his head, eyed her. "I don't remember telling you exactly why I quit."

"Yeah. I figured it out. But you loved your job, and you were good at it. Sometimes things beyond our control go wrong. It wasn't your fault."

Wasn't it?

He sighed. Watched for that someone Olivia believed was following them, if he existed.

Olivia. Always the nurturer. He looked down at her. Even in her disheveled state, she was beautiful, with her coppery brown locks and cinnamon eyes that swirled with warmth and compassion. He wanted to curl into her, envelop her. Instead, he lifted a strand of her hair and even that small touch made him weak in the knees.

Dropping the hair, he turned back to gassing up the truck. "Thanks for your words."

But they'd brought back the images he wanted to forget.

"Detective Long. You recognize my voice?"

"Jimmy Delaney."

Jimmy had taken Sarah that day. And when Zach had heard the gunfire over the phone, he'd thought that had been the end of his sister. That there would be no negotiation for her and this was simple revenge. Payback for the shot Zach had fired that had killed Jimmy's brother when he'd come to arrest Jimmy. But Jimmy had wanted more.

Sarah's subsequent scream in the background and sobs had let him know the man hadn't killed her right there and then, though Zach would have expected no less of him.

"That was to let you know I mean business. Your sister is alive. I'll trade her for you. So come alone. I can smell a cop a mile away. I don't want any pigs within a five-mile radius. Nobody knows about this or she dies. Bring your police father and they both die. Am I clear?"

Zach hesitated, his mind in a rushing panic to figure out how to save his sister and come out alive, too, if possible.

"Am. I. Clear?" Jimmy shouted over the phone.

"Crystal."

Jimmy sounded off instructions and gave Zach ten minutes to get there. He was fifteen minutes away from that location.

Ten minutes! No time to call for backup or explain the situation and the need for complete silence on police radios. He was supposed to come alone.

And that was it, then. He would go alone. Do as Jimmy commanded and hope Sarah would walk away with her life. He held out no hope for his own.

He rushed to his car and drove like a maniac, conscious that drawing the attention of a traffic cop would thwart his efforts.

But on the way...on the way, he'd called for backup. The training was in his blood, and he couldn't change that now. His father's words, after years of policing the city—always call for backup—*wouldn't leave him in this crisis.*

So he'd done what he was supposed to do. Jimmy Delaney couldn't be allowed to call the shots. And then he was there, facing off with Jimmy. Sarah was set to step outside to her freedom and run to safety.

Zach was ready to die for her, and he would if backup didn't come.

Except for that one siren. That one stupid police siren. Jimmy aimed at Sarah's back and fired. Then he turned the weapon on Zach.

He'd woken up in the hospital.

They'd get Cooper, his father and the sheriff involved, but not until he and Olivia were somewhat safe, far away from here. He'd keep her close and protect her and when this was over, they'd walk away from each other. Those flashes of memory, like being near Olivia, made him weak, and he couldn't afford to be weak. Not now.

SEVENTEEN

Olivia had never been so glad to be home.

Home.

Was Gideon really her home now?

Zach returned to the same parking spot from which he'd retrieved his truck. Before he got out, he faced her, agony in his features. "I don't know what to do now."

Second-guessing himself again? Instead of being strong and demanding and authoritative and telling her what to do, he was being…vulnerable. This was a side to him she hadn't seen in much too long.

Was he asking her what she wanted to do? What she thought? First she had to better understand his uncertainty. "What do you mean? We go in and get the thumb drive."

"I want to put you somewhere safe while I finish this, but I'm not sure I trust anyone as much as myself to keep you safe."

She smiled at that. "Glad to hear you see the truth. There's no doubt for me. You're the *only* person I trust to keep us safe." He frowned at that. She'd hoped for a different reaction. "You don't believe me?"

"No, it's not that. I'm not sure why I would even trust

myself for the job. I don't want to make a mistake, make the wrong decision. So that's why I'm asking you what you want to do. Once I have that thumb drive in my possession, I'll be a walking dead man—like that's much different from now—until I turn it over to someone in authority who can use it to bring justice. We need to touch base with Cooper and see if he can get a hold of his father. See if the man will even meet with us. A lot can happen between now and then."

She glanced through the truck windows to see if she could find who had followed them, that sensation still buzzing through her like she was some sort of radar detector. "That's the case with the sheriff, too. Let's get somewhere safe and warm, then call him. Looks like the phones are charged and good to go now. And then, Zach, we wait."

"Wait?"

Olivia turned her gaze back to Zach and hoped he would listen.

"We wait for Cooper's father to contact someone or we wait for Sheriff Kruse. Whoever gets here first, gets to open that locker. I don't want you bearing this burden anymore. It was never yours, but my brother brought you in because he trusted you. He thought you were law enforcement, and as far as I'm concerned you still are. It's in your blood. You're just...between jobs. So I want you to think like a policeman now. Be who you've always been on the inside—sworn to protect."

He smiled then, and she hadn't seen that in so long, she soaked it up like the sunshine when the skies cleared after a long, gray winter.

"You're too good to me, Olivia. Talking sense into me. I don't deserve it." He opened the truck door and rushed around to assist her out. A gentleman. He grabbed her waist and instead of lifting her down—though she needed no help—he leaned in closer.

The scent of him wrapped around her and made her dizzy. Memories swirled in her heart and mind and erased the ten years that had gone by—she and Zach were in love once again. Only this time no obstacles—resentment, time or distance—rose between them.

"What are you doing?" she whispered, her throat thick with emotion, her tone challenging him to back off. But she didn't want him to move. *God, help me...*she didn't want him to move even one inch away from her.

She grabbed his collar to prevent him from stepping away. He inched closer, his face mere millimeters from hers. Her heart screamed for him to kiss her, but her mind resounded with warnings. "We can't go back, Zach. You know that." Oh, why had she spoken and broken the moment?

But the moment remained. Zach remained.

"No, we can't," he said.

Then his lips were against hers in a tender, gentle, sweet kiss that spoke of promises neither of them would keep. They couldn't. She tasted her salty tears and he had to taste them, too, then he inched away.

"I never got to kiss you goodbye. I just wanted one more kiss. So, after ten years, I'm taking that kiss now."

"You didn't take it. I gave it, willingly." Breathless, she edged back and away.

Kissing him had been risky. Dangerous. Her thoughts were all muddled when she needed to focus on the next few moments and hours. She needed to think about Rich. Was he alive or dead? "Can we call Ranger Taggart now to ask about Rich?"

She stepped out of the truck completely and shut the door. A scuffle behind her drew her attention. Zach lay sprawled on the ground. And a big brute of a man stood in his place.

Pain split his skull as light shattered his eyesight. Grabbing his head, Zach groaned. Once the fog cleared from his thoughts, the panic set in. He sat up and brushed the cold snow off. His truck still rested there in the parking lot. No one else was there to witness what'd happened.

Olivia.

"Olivia!"

Where was she?

One moment she was getting out of the truck as he waited. They'd shared a kiss. One forbidden kiss—but they were both consenting adults and knew it was their last. The kiss could take them nowhere…it was more about closure.

And then pain struck him like a bolt from the sky. Darkness enveloped him.

His cell phone rang, bringing him back to reality, his terrifying reality. The new phone.

Nobody had this number except Rich, Olivia and Ranger Taggart.

Dread flooded his heart as he glanced at the caller ID.

Olivia.

He answered. "Hello?"

"Detective Long," a gruff voice replied. "Oh, wait, you're no longer a detective."

Anger and fear twisted together. "Who is this?" *Where's Olivia?* But Zach was afraid to say her name. To demand her whereabouts. He was afraid if he said her name, then he would be voicing his worst fears and the guy was sure to hear that fear right through the cell phone and use it against him.

He already was.

"You don't know me. It doesn't matter."

"Then what do you want? Why are you calling?" But Zach knew.

Please, God, let me be wrong. Let me be wrong!

"Shut up and listen."

Remaining quiet, Zach waited for the man's instructions, desperately trying to push aside a replay of the past.

"This can only go well for you if you do exactly what I say. Get that thumb drive of the video and bring it to me. Then I'll let her go. I'll let her live."

Sweat broke out over Zach, despite the winter chill. The man was lying, but he couldn't challenge him over the phone. Not with her life on the line. He'd been through this before and it had ended in the worst possible way. Squeezing his eyes closed, he shut those images from his mind. Olivia's life depended on him. He had to have tunnel vision. Focus on one thing.

Saving her.

"Are you still there?" the man asked.

Too wrapped in terror and dread, Zach had failed to respond. "Yes."

"One more thing."

"What's that?" But he heard the answer in his head before the man told him.

"Come alone. I see anyone else, anything at all suspicious, I'll kill her and take what I want from you anyway. You know I can do it."

This can't be happening again.

Zach couldn't breathe. Phone still pressed to his ear, he

dropped to his knees in the snow. He sucked in a breath, and then another. Swiped at the sweat pouring over his brow and composed himself. Focused on what he had to do. Be strong for Olivia. Save her. But everything in him was unraveling and he had no power to change it.

God, help me now! When I am weak You are strong. If You're not strong for me now, then I don't know what I'm going to do!

An image of Olivia's face came into focus. Her coppery hair that smelled of sweet strawberries and eyes that lit with humor, sparked with determination and softened when nurturing. His pulse throbbed and for a moment, he thought he would die right there. But then his heart surged with a fierce love for her that, at this, his weakest moment, he had no strength to bury away.

She's counting on you. She's going to die if you don't do this right!

"Let me hear her so I know she's alive."

A scuffling sound and then, "Zach?" Olivia tried to sound strong and brave, but he knew her too well, could hear the terror threading through her voice. "Please—" A scream erupted from her.

"Olivia!" He yelled into the phone.

"Convinced?"

"Don't you touch her. Don't you lay a finger on her, or I'll—"

"What? You'll what?" The man ground out his words, cutting Zach off.

Helpless, impotent, Zach would comply, and this man knew it. "I'll get what you want. Just tell me where to meet you. And Olivia had better be there front and center or I'll turn around and make sure the whole world knows." *What you did...*

Knowing what they knew, his and Olivia's lives were already forfeit. Again, he was left with no real choices.

"Listen… I'm not a bad guy in the true sense of the words. I'm just trying to make the world a safer place, and sometimes there's collateral damage. Don't make this any worse than it has to be."

The man's words, his plea of pseudo innocence, surprised Zach. Nausea rolled through him. He had plenty of harsh words he'd love to spew at the moment, but he held his tongue for now. This man would be served justice in good time, and Zach would set Olivia free, even if it cost his life. Any other outcome was unthinkable. "Just tell me where and when."

His heart sank deeper as he listened to the instructions.

The location was forty-five minutes away.

Zach had thirty minutes to be there with the thumb drive in hand.

EIGHTEEN

Olivia still lay on the floor where the big man had shoved her.

"Zach!" she screamed just as the man ended the call.

Fear boiled inside and pushed its way up, ready to explode in sobs, but she shoved them back down. She would not let this man see her cry. She wouldn't tremble or whimper when he stared her down.

His name was Michael Key, founder of KeyCorp, and Rich's boss before he'd fled. She'd learned that much.

She pressed her back against the farthest wall. She didn't want to be anywhere near him, but in this small and empty cabin where he'd brought her, she had no choice. When she'd spotted Zach on the ground, his form splayed out, she'd screamed. Was he dead or simply unconscious? The guy had pressed his weapon so hard into her coat she could feel the muzzle against her rib cage, and he'd told her to shut up or die.

She'd complied.

He then dragged her over to another vehicle and forced her inside. Had driven her here to this empty house so he could threaten her for the location of the thumb drive. Though terrified, she somehow kept calm when she explained to him she didn't have it, nor did she know where it was. A half lie. He hadn't believed her and slapped her. Olivia had almost been reduced to whimpers.

How could she stand strong when she didn't even know if Zach was alive or dead? Rich either.

Mr. Key huffed. Paced the room as if angry about his conversation with Zach. Olivia shoved to her feet. That drew his glare.

"Why have you sent men to kill us, to kill Rich, if you wanted that thumb drive? How would you get it if you killed us?"

Fire burned in his eyes. Olivia thought she might just whimper after all.

"I didn't know about it, that's why. But we caught up with Rich's friend who left with him. In order to save his own skin, Jonathan was quick to tell us what Rich had taken. So mission parameters changed. I need Rich alive. Or someone who can get me the thumb drive."

Olivia averted her gaze. *And you let Jonathan live?* Afraid of the answer, she didn't voice the question.

"You should be glad your boyfriend woke up to answer the call."

At least he was alive and well, but now he would have to do the impossible.

And worse…Key was using Olivia against Zach to get what he wanted. Just like a criminal had used Zach's sister to get what he wanted—which happened to be Zach himself. Losing his sister like that had almost destroyed Zach. It had destroyed his career. She couldn't allow herself to be used in this way.

God, please, show me what to do!

Because of what Zach went through with Sarah, he would get the thumb drive and bring it to this man in order to save Olivia's life. But he had to know there was no way they would be left alive to tell this story. Handing over the information would only mean their deaths. The criminals would remain free to commit their crimes. Zach would do what he had to do, but Olivia must come up with something, whatever she could, to stop this. All of it. But what?

"He can't make it here in time, you know that. It took you forty-five minutes from Gideon. Zach still has to find the thumb drive and this place. You gave him an impossible mission. Why?"

"So he won't have time to make a copy once he has it."

Maybe Rich already had. Had this man thought of that? Probably, but she wouldn't bring it up. Maybe this was just the beginning of a drawn-out search for any other copies made of the video.

"He won't have time to get here either."

He didn't respond to that but paced the room, his forbidding presence and marine-sized body making the small living space even smaller.

"I didn't want things to come to this." He waved his gun around.

"What do you mean?" Olivia didn't want to engage him in conversation but on the other hand, she wanted answers. "You didn't want to kill us?"

"That's what I mean."

"You sure have a strange way of showing it, since we've been running from shooters since the beginning. Like I'm going to believe what you told Zach, that you would let us live once you had the thumb drive."

Key scowled. Things hadn't gone like he'd hoped or planned, that much appeared obvious.

"So…what happened?" She wouldn't bother to think

that learning more could be dangerous. If she didn't escape she was already dead.

He arched a brow. "Don't bother trying to convince me you don't know anything."

"I don't know much, but what's your side of the story?"

"Things got out of hand. It all happened too quickly and when it was over, we knew we could never explain our way out of the bloodbath. The thing is, Rich is just as guilty as anyone. He is just as likely to be tried and convicted. Your brother should have left well enough alone."

He glanced out the window and watched the woods, then turned to her, his eyes dark. "But now? Now he's involved others. If you want to blame anyone, blame him for what we've had to do here."

Suddenly he marched toward her. Olivia pressed against the wall, wishing she could walk through it and disappear.

Chambering a round in his weapon, he looked at her. "If you try anything, you know I have no compunction against harming you. Killing you if I have to. Do you understand?"

She nodded more vehemently than she would have liked. She didn't want him to know just how terrified she was. But maybe she was fooling herself to think he didn't already understand the depth of her fear.

He grabbed her arm. "Let's go."

He dragged her through the cabin. "Go? Where are we going?"

But he didn't answer. Once inside his SUV, she glanced into the back and spotted a… "Is that… What is that?"

"A drone."

"Are you kidding me?"

As he glanced over his shoulder a grin slid into his cheek.

"Did you… Is that how you found us? You followed us with that?"

"It's a Raven. Specifically, an AeroVironment RQ-11 Raven. I made a few modifications myself. What do you think my company does? We provide security. We monitor. We perform reconnaissance."

What had Rich been thinking? Why had he thought he could ever escape?

Key glanced her way again, a smirk on his lips. "You never had a chance."

Sweaty palm gripping the cell phone in his pocket, Zach wanted to crush it as he entered the Wilderness, Inc. snowmobile rental cabin. Pushing through the door he noticed several people renting snowmobiles. He slowed his pace and kept his head down, glancing up enough to orient to the business and where he could find the lockers. Then he made a beeline for them, situated in a space at the back. Didn't have time for questions or conversation.

Once he had the thumb drive in hand, he might try to call for backup—the Wilde siblings would be the most expedient—but he hadn't decided on that yet.

Hadn't Sarah lost her life because a police officer, one of his brothers against crime, had turned on his siren, signaling law enforcement's approach and alerting Jimmy Delaney that Zach had called for backup?

Heart pounding, he jogged past the lockers, a man on a race against time.

Five, ten, twenty...thirty-two.

Locker thirty-two.

This was it.

Before they'd left the ranger station, Rich had been able to give him the locker number and the combination. Zach had memorized the simple addition fact. Seven plus six equals thirteen. Pulse roaring in his ears, he reached for the lock. He turned three times to the right. Seven. Then all the way around to thirteen. Then back to six, but his fingers slipped.

He groaned. "I don't have time for this!"

He stared at his trembling hands. *Get a grip, man.* Olivia's life was on the line.

Sucking in a breath, he tried the combination again. And again.

Breath hitching, he closed his eyes and took a few calming breaths.

Please, God, could You give me some help here?

Another breath and he opened his eyes. His gaze fell on the locker number. He was at number thirty-three, not thirty-two. What? How had that happened? He shifted to the right locker and still got nowhere.

Oh, for crying out loud. What am I doing wrong? He was at the right locker. Had Rich given him the wrong combination? A tall slender guy in his late teens who reminded Zach of Shaggy from Scooby-Doo walked in drinking a soda.

"Hey, can I have that can?" Zach asked. "I'm in a hurry and need to get into my locker."

The guy eyed him. "Get your own."

Zach pulled out his gun. "Sorry, dude, a life is on the line and I need your soda."

The man dropped the soda can, carbonated liquid fizzing out on the floor, and lifted his hands in the air. "Sure, okay, whatever you say."

"It's an emergency. Can you help me?"

Arching a brow, the man dropped his hands. "I don't know."

Zach put his weapon back, feeling like an idiot. He emptied the rest of the soda in the garbage can. "Got a knife on you?"

Wild-eyed, the kid backed up against the lockers. "What are you going to do?"

"Listen, I used to be a police officer. I have a friend in trouble. I have to get into this locker. Now are you going to help me or not? And…I'm sorry I pulled a gun on you." Illegal. Totally illegal, but he was desperate.

The kid nodded and pulled a Buck knife from his pocket.

"Thanks." Zach pushed away all morbid thoughts and focused on creating a shim.

Once he'd cut the shim out of the can, he crouched closer to the lock and worked the shim into the inside of the shackle and the lock. Then he pinched the shim and popped the shackle.

The combination lock opened up.

"Wow, it's like watching those old episodes of MacGyver."

"Are you telling me you never forgot your combination before?" And that made him wonder why Rich would use such an easy-to-break-open lock for such crucial information. Still, if no one knew what was inside the locker, it didn't matter.

"Should you be opening that locker, Mister? Is it even yours?" A new voice boomed from behind.

"You don't seem like the kind of guy to forget his combination." Shaggy this time.

Zach huffed a laugh. Stood tall and faced Gray Wilde. The man's eyes widened in surprise. "Zach. I wasn't expecting to see you. I heard someone waved a gun around back here and broke into a locker."

"Yeah, it was cool." Shaggy grinned.

Gray stared, waiting for his explanation. Now came the moment he hadn't wanted to face. Should he tell Gray about Olivia? If he did would it cost her life when he didn't come alone?

"I'm in a hurry. Had to get into Rich's locker." He opened it and found the small thumb drive just sitting there on the top shelf of the mostly empty locker.

"What's going on, Zach? Where's Olivia?"

The question he didn't want to answer, and yet he knew he needed help to save her.

With his back still to Gray, he exhaled long and hard until his shoulders dropped. He had a job to do. Just one thing. All he had to do was take this information to where that man held Olivia and hand it over. In his dreams, he would pull her into his arms and hold her safe and sound. But the man hadn't given Zach enough time to begin with. Now he would never make it.

He slammed the locker shut and pushed past Gray, who followed him outside.

"I can't talk now. He's holding Olivia. Wants to trade her for this. I have to go alone. Now get out of my way."

Gray yanked him around so hard he nearly stumbled and fell on the icy ground. "What are you talking about? You can't go into this alone. You need backup, man. Where's your training?"

Zach scowled. "Haven't you heard the story? My sister died because I called for backup."

"Look, I'm sorry to hear about that. I don't know what happened then, but you walk into this alone and you are both dead. These people aren't going to let you live. You know that! Now, where are you headed?"

Running through the snow, he made it to his truck, Gray on his heels. How did he lose the guy? He spouted off the location he'd been given to appease Gray.

"I know the cabin."

"Good, then you can pick up the pieces after it's over, but in the meantime just stay away."

"Zach, you can't be serious."

"I'm dead serious. As long as Olivia walks out alive, that's all that matters to me."

NINETEEN

Olivia looked for an opportunity to jump out of the SUV as the man drove toward their meeting place, but then what? More running through the woods and fighting snowstorms to stay alive? Being shot at? His weapon rested on the console, pointing at her with his hand over it, finger near the trigger guard.

She wouldn't get far.

As strange as it seemed, it was almost a relief that they were finally at this part of this trial—and she would face the end, one way or another.

Key steered to the side of the road. A couple of cars passed. He shifted into Park and glared at her, then looked at his cell phone. "Gotta make a call before I lose this signal."

He hit the number then pressed the phone to his left ear. Olivia glanced out her window. If she was going to make a run for it, now would be the moment. She fidgeted, her hand inching up the door to the handle. A knot grew in her throat. She tried to act normal—right, what was normal in this situation?—and glanced over to him.

He held the weapon up and pointed it at her, anticipating her move. Olivia held his gaze. Could she reason with him? Then someone answered the cell on the other end.

Zach's voice echoed from the phone into the cab. Her heart longed to be free, to be in his arms. Why had she ever denied herself loving again, loving that man? If she had it all to do over…

No, this wasn't about a redo of the past. If she had another chance at life, another chance with him, she would build a new life, a future with him. That was, if he would have her.

"You didn't give me enough time!" Zach shouted, but then, more controlled and measured, "I just now have my hands on the thumb drive. Not to mention, I'm not going to have cell reception so you can't call me again. I'm on my way. If you want to see this thumb drive you'd better give me Olivia alive and well and unharmed."

It was just as she'd feared. Her pulse roared in her ears making it hard to hear the rest of what he said.

"Change of venue," Key said. "We're meeting at Olivia's house. You have twenty-five minutes."

"What?" Zach shouted.

The brute ended the call.

"What are you doing?" Olivia asked as he steered back onto the road. Did he realize that would be a crime scene, possibly taped off by now? But maybe that was his strategy. Nobody would think to look for them there. "He'll have to go back and get a snowmobile. Are you crazy? Why delay the meeting?"

"It's not a delay. I'm shaking things up in case he made plans to have others meet us. They won't have time to get there. And he can make it if he turns around now."

She sat in silence, grappling to comprehend her circumstances. What if Zach didn't make it? And what would happen if he did?

Olivia wasn't ready to die. Not like this.

God, please, save us! I want a second chance. I'm sorry if I'm asking too much here. People all around me are suffering and dying all the time. But I don't want to die. Help me to be brave. Save Zach, if nothing else... save him.

Dread shuddered through her core, and she fought to stifle her whimpers.

"I know what you're thinking," he said. "It's a crime scene now and law enforcement will be crawling all over the place. But nobody is at the house. I can see what's happening on my iPhone through the little cameras I put in strategic locations."

He lifted his phone so she could see the image. Sure enough her house sat alone and empty.

"The sheriff's in Gold Beach along with the hunters they rescued. See, I'm not such a bad guy. They're alive. They offered my men food and shelter, though believe me, my men had come prepared for anything, including inclement weather. But their move was strategic. They took the hunters' clothes and tied them up and left them in their camp so they would be safe and warm and alive until someone found them."

Pressing her head against the seat back she closed her eyes. At least they had been found alive and well, if she could believe this man. Maybe the hunters had escaped with their lives, but they didn't know about the cover-up, and she held out no such hope for her and Zach. She needed a plan to save them. Though she trusted Zach to be a hero, this was more than a single man could handle on his own. Had he called for backup? Called the sheriff or told Cooper and Gray? Considering Zach's history, she doubted it.

He would try to save her on his own.

He would risk his life, if that was what it took. Olivia couldn't let him do that. This guy, he'd thought it all out, planned everything to the last detail. Even stopped to trade his SUV for a snowmobile he'd parked for this moment. They'd need to ride it in order to get to her house. He pressed the weapon under her chin, terrifying her.

"Let me make it perfectly clear that I will shoot you dead if you try to escape me. And when your boyfriend comes to me with the thumb drive, I will kill him, too."

Tears burned, hot and salty, sliding over her cold cheeks. *You're not going to let us live.*

And then a plan came to her. It was risky, but it was all she had.

Ten minutes later, the man who abducted her steered up next to her house on the snowmobile. The house sat alone and serene, again reminding her of a Thomas Kinkade picture. Like nothing horrific had happened to the inhabitants. Things were often not what they seemed, as was certainly the case here. And it felt like ages ago since she'd welcomed Rich into the home, surprising him that she was even there, but it had only been four days. Ages ago since she'd run into Zach looking for him. And yet, it had only been three of the longest days of her life.

Her breathing hitched up. She thought she would hyperventilate.

You're going to die if you don't do something. It's a huge risk, but you're going to die.

You have to act.

Now.

You have to do something now.

Key slid from the snowmobile. Waved his weapon at her as he removed his helmet.

A branch snapped behind him, distracting him for

one millisecond. Snow fell in clumps. Now. Now was her chance. Olivia dashed behind a tree and then around to the back of the house. She knew her way around these woods, unlike this man.

He fired off his weapon. "I'm going to kill your boyfriend as soon as I see him if you don't come back! You hear me?"

Oh, God, please no!

Was she doing the right thing by escaping?

Had she just cost Zach his life by running?

From behind a cedar tree she waited, catching her breath though fear tried to choke her. The man's cursing resounded, muted by snow-covered evergreens, and grew louder. She'd been waiting to see if he would come for her.

Now, to lead him away from Zach without getting shot and killed.

Olivia shoved from the tree and ran for her life, keeping to the thickest trunks for cover. Bullets shattered the bark near her head. But she kept running through the snow, hoping her heart didn't give out with the fear and effort.

In the distance, she spotted hers, Rich's and Zach's snowmobiles left from days ago when everything had started. She slid down the incline, the slope that led to the nearly frozen brook she and Zach had followed. She had this chance. This one chance. There was no other way out of this. Either he would follow her or he would kill them both once Zach arrived with the thumb drive. Then the criminal would go free.

And if Rich wasn't already dead from his wounds, they would find him and kill him, after all. Finally, she stopped behind a fallen tree that had crumbled into a clump of wood covered in snow. She waited until she caught her breath, calmed her heart, then listened.

A branch cracked somewhere above her and snow slid from the crown, like what had distracted Key for the moment she'd needed.

Thank You, God.

She hoped and prayed the man had followed her. She'd needed to stay ahead of him enough so he couldn't shoot her, but then again, she'd wanted him to follow.

"You hear me?" he hollered.

Yep. He'd followed. In a few minutes Zach would arrive at the house and find it empty. She had to hurry or it would be too late. As if to confirm her fears, the whir of a snowmobile resounded in the distance.

Zach. Oh, Zach...

For his sake, she had to end this, once and for all. She couldn't be traded for the thumb drive even if it were possible Michael Key would let her live, but it wasn't.

Cold seeped through her clothes, slid deep into her lungs and burned her cheeks. She pushed from the tree.

"I hear you! I'm not letting you trade me for the thumb drive. You'll never get your hands on it." There. That taunt should draw the man in her direction instead of toward Zach who held the dangerous information close.

Pushing from the tree, she slogged through the thick snow, her limbs burning with the exertion.

Finally...finally, she came to the edge of the deadly crevice. The drop, a crack in the earth where she hoped to lure him to his death.

He slowed as he drew near the house. It appeared empty. But how could he know? Still, Zach kept his distance, revved the snowmobile. Had he been heard? Did the guy expect him to march up to the porch and knock on the door? He'd do that if he had no other choice.

The way he'd imagined things going down, two people should be exiting the house about now. In that case, Zach would get off this machine and walk toward Olivia, let her walk past him and toward the snowmobile. Once she'd driven off, he'd toss the thumb drive into the snow. Let the man find it.

He had no illusions about walking away unscathed, unharmed, or even living.

God, please, just let me get Olivia out alive. Can You just let this one thing...this one thing...work right in my life? Turn out as I hoped and planned? It's not wrong to pray for her life, and more than that, I don't know what You want from me.

Except maybe trust. After everything he'd been through, asking Zach to trust was too much.

A minute passed. Then two. Zach frowned. He'd have to get off this machine. He hopped off and jogged to the house. Pounded on the door. It swung open.

Dark and stale.

Empty.

Still, he'd check it thoroughly. After looking in every room, he knew that no one had even gone inside.

Panic engulfed him.

He tugged out his cell phone in case the guy had tried to call, but with no stable signal, Zach wouldn't have received the call. The man would know that. In fact, he couldn't have made a call if he was in the area.

Snowmobile tracks led in and a machine sat at the side of the house. So someone had recently come here. Zach exited the back door, hiked over to the snowmobile and pressed his hand against it. Still warm. Then he saw two sets of footprints.

Was this a replay of the day he'd first arrived at the house? Except they were on foot this time.

Then he heard it. A voice. Someone yelling in the woods.

And gunfire.

He glanced from the house to the woods. Had Olivia escaped?

Could God be answering his prayers, only in a different way? Zach would ride his snowmobile to catch up with them. He followed the tracks as best he could and neared the three machines from two days ago left to be buried in the snow. The fresh tracks led away and down the slope.

No.

Oh, no! He had a feeling he knew what Olivia planned. He didn't need to follow them down into the brook. He already knew what she was doing, where she was leading her captor, if he hadn't already caught up. By the looks of their tracks, he had been behind her all the way.

Zach should call to him, distract him, pull him away from Olivia if it wasn't too late. Then again he'd probably heard the snowmobile and was expecting Zach. There was nothing else to be done. If he had any chance of making it in time, before they reached the crevice, he had to ride and give away his approach.

It was all or nothing.

The trees grew thicker in places, forcing him to slow.

No, no, no, no…he didn't want to get stuck. This was no groomed trail.

He had to make it there in time.

"Olivia! No!" He couldn't help himself. He shouted the warning to her.

And then, in the distance through the trees, he spotted a man.

Olivia just stood there. If Zach judged it correctly, she was at the edge of the gulch. Zach's heart pounded. His limbs raged, urging the snowmobile forward, faster over the snow.

He could make it. He could do this.

Except the man's time was up. He lunged for her.

And Olivia…disappeared into the fissure.

TWENTY

Olivia clung to a root growing through the bedrock, her feet hanging over the long, deadly drop. With gloves that were slippery inside, her hands ached as she squeezed the root, holding on for her life.

Key hadn't followed her in. He hadn't fallen to his death, even though he'd reached for her. She'd known the root from a nearby pine thrust out at that spot. Had anticipated grabbing it. But this had been a huge risk. Her only chance to save Zach, if not herself.

Her heart hammered against her rib cage fighting to get out. She could only imagine the horror Zach must feel at the moment, believing that she'd fallen into the fissure. She'd heard his shout, his rage, muted as it echoed down into the fissure.

"Zach!" She climbed up the root and made it to the ledge.

He'd drawn Key's attention completely and the man fired his semiautomatic weapon at the underside of a snowmobile as it flew through the air.

A scream erupted from her throat. Zach's body left the machine and slammed into the big ex-military man even as the vehicle hit the snow. The impact knocked Key to the ground.

Zach scrambled to his feet and then straddled the man, holding his own weapon to his face. "I told you if you touched her, if you laid a hand on her again, I was going to—"

"Zach!" she shouted.

But he didn't turn away and lose his focus on the man. Just kept the weapon aimed at him point-blank. Puffs of white filled the air, telling her how hard he breathed. Michael Key, too.

Good. Let him be terrified now.

"I'm okay. Just…don't kill him. You don't have to kill him now."

"I thought…"

"I know, and I'm sorry."

He pulled the thumb drive from his pocket and dangled it in front of the man. "I'm not going to kill you. But God knows I want to. He knows it, so no point in me hiding it. But you're going down. You and everyone involved."

Would that mean Rich, too? Her heart ached.

More snowmobiles resounded in the distance.

"Is that? Did you—"

"Call for backup?" He finished her sentence.

That surprised her, but she was glad to hear it.

"No. But Gray was there. He lent me the snowmobile. He knew what was going down."

Sagging in relief, she risked moving a few steps closer as they waited for the others to arrive. Relief whooshed through her at the sight of Sheriff Kruse, Cooper, Gray and two others. They took Michael Key into custody, relieving Zach. He stumbled away, then turned.

Zach stopped and stared at her.

His icy blue gaze swept her form, then held her gaze.

What she saw there—pain, regret and…hope, knocked into her and kept her anchored in the snow. He hiked forward, closing the distance, but stopped just short of wrapping his arms around her.

"I thought you were gone." Still, he stood there staring her down. "Why did you do it?"

"I couldn't let him kill you. Kill us. We had no chance and you know it. Not unless I ran. Not unless I could lead him to the fissure. Only, he didn't fall in like I did. Like I planned."

Deep frown lines creased his forehead, furrowed his brows. "Don't ever do that again."

"What? Try to save you?"

He stepped closer. "I don't need saving."

"No, you don't. Any more than I need protecting. That's just it. I do need protection and you protected me. More than that. You saved me, Zach. This time, you saved someone you…" *Loved.* She gasped. Exhaled slowly. He didn't love her anymore. That was long ago, and yet, when she looked in his eyes, she could see it plainly now just as she'd seen it ten years ago.

"What were you going to say? Finish it."

"I don't know what I was going to say."

A smile tugged at the corner of his lips. Zach brushed her cold cheeks with his hand. "I never stopped, you know?"

"Stopped what?" Her legs trembled. Was it from the cold? She couldn't be sure.

Zach didn't have the chance to answer. Sheriff Kruse approached and interrupted them. "We need to get our prisoner back. I'll have to get statements from you, too, but first you'll need a ride, won't you?" Nodding at Olivia, he said, "It's best to finish this conversation back where you're safe and warm."

Olivia followed the sheriff and climbed onto a snowmobile behind Zach, slipping her arms around him. She pressed her face against his back and soaked in a living, breathing Zach. The man she had always loved. She'd almost lost him again, only this time for good. But he wasn't hers now, not really. Once this was over he would go his way and she would go…somewhere else.

Behind them, Cooper and Gray rode together, and a handcuffed Michael Key now rode with the sheriff. One of the other two strangers looked an awful lot like Cooper and Gray. Their father?

Rich! Her thoughts turned to her brother. She had to find out if he was okay. Ranger Taggart, too. They could still be in danger!

Two days later, Zach began to wonder if he would ever get a moment alone with Olivia. A guy named Jefferson from the Department of Justice, a contact brought in by Cooper's father, Ethan Wilde, had repeatedly grilled them. Olivia had been right. The man did have connections and there had been no fear the wrong people would hear the news and push things quietly aside.

But through all of it, they'd been kept apart. Maybe he didn't deserve another chance with Olivia.

He sighed, desperation flooding his mind and heart. That's what he got for letting her back in.

Liv...

But he couldn't worry about that now as he walked with Sheriff Kruse to Rich's hospital room. He'd make sure he got a chance to talk to Olivia. Last time, when things ended for them, he'd wanted to go back to talk it through one more time, should have gone back. Maybe it would all have been different.

This time, he would make sure he talked it out with her, talked it through. See what's what. He'd make sure he got his chance.

Sheriff Kruse pushed the door open and held it for Zach. Rich had finally been moved from ICU and recovered from his injuries. Ranger Taggart had kept Rich safe until additional park LEOs—law enforcement officers—had arrived, searched the woods for other shooters and apprehended them, and delivered Rich to the hospital.

Relieved to see his friend recovering, Zach moved to his bedside, acknowledging that Olivia stood on the other side. He wanted to stand next to her and hold her hand, but he focused on Rich now.

"Hey, buddy." Zach gripped his hand. "You made it. We made it."

"Yeah." Rich huffed a laugh. "I wasn't sure we were going to make it out alive. And I think this guy Jefferson, I think he's going to do something about what happened. It's not going to go away quietly. And who knows, maybe I'll even be charged—"

"Rich, no," Olivia whispered. "You're the whistle-blower, that's all. You risked your life to get the truth out."

"Yeah, but I risked more than my life. I risked your lives, too. And I'm sorry. I never meant for things to go the way they did."

"You couldn't have known," Zach said.

"Well, anyway. I'm sorry I dragged you into this."

"I'm not." Olivia moved away from Rich to look out the window.

Both Zach and Rich jerked their gazes to her. "You're

not sorry you were dragged into this and almost lost your life?" Zach asked.

Had she lost her mind? Zach didn't want to hold anything against Rich, but he was close, so close, to doing just that.

She whirled from the window. "I'm not sorry at all. You're back, Rich. And Rich brought you back into our lives, Zach."

Her gaze locked with Zach's.

A nurse entered the room to check Rich's vitals. He yawned. "I think I need to rest now."

What? Zach caught Rich's wink. Yeah. Totally faking it.

"Come on, Olivia, let's give the guy some time to recover. Remember, he's back now. Before you know it you'll wish he was out of your hair." He made sure to inject a humorous tone into his sarcasm.

He ushered her out of the room and took her hand in his. She didn't object. Zach needed to find some place quiet and private. He had to finish his conversation with her.

He had to know.

And for two days he hadn't had access to her. That had driven him crazy.

But he couldn't find the perfect place in this hospital. Nor did he have the patience to wait. Still, he walked her into a corner and pressed his arms on either side of her, in essence trapping her. He gazed into her cinnamon eyes—warmth swirled with alarm—and lifted a strand of her soft, coppery brown hair. He didn't have to get any closer to smell the strawberry scent.

"What are you doing?" Her voice sounded thick with emotion.

"We need to finish our conversation. You know, the one we started on the mountain."

"You mean the one where you said you had never stopped?"

"Yeah, that's the one."

Her chest rose and fell with anticipation. Or was it panic. "I've been dying to ask you what you were going to say."

"So. Go ahead. Ask."

"What, Zach? You never stopped what?"

He wasn't sure she wanted to hear. That she really wanted to know, considering she had kept saying they could never go back. But he took a chance. A big fat chance. He leaned in close, until his lips were almost on hers—because he couldn't help himself.

This close, her essence wrapped around him urging him closer, but he kept his distance until the right moment.

"I never stopped loving you," he whispered softy, tenderly. "I hid it away. Ran from it. I was so hurt. But that love I had for you before we split, it burrowed in and grew. It didn't die like I thought. Seeing you again, going through this with you, opened that door wide."

"But we can't go back. You know that."

They were back to that again. But Zach would forge ahead. He had nothing, literally nothing, to lose.

"Forget about the past. I don't want to go back. I want to go forward, and I want you with me here and now. With me at this moment, in the present. With me in my future."

He should have waited for her reply, but he was too afraid of the rejection. He couldn't take losing her a second time. So he pressed his lips against hers, warm and soft at first, then slipped his arms around her, bringing her closer. Breathed in the scent of her. How had he ever let her go? He'd come to a place where he would have died for her.

Why had it been so hard to live for her?

Her salty tears met his lips again.

But he wasn't finished. He had to close the deal and seal it. Though he could have stayed there with her in his arms forever, he eased back just far enough to see her face. "Tell me you love me, too."

Her warm eyes, swirled with brown sugar this time, gazed into his. "I love you more now, Zach. I don't want to waste any more of my life away from you. If you want to be a police officer, a detective, I don't care. I love you."

He grinned, never more thrilled in his life than in hearing those words. "Are you sure? Because if you're not, then I'll do something else, but I've been thinking about becoming a park ranger. We could stay here, live in the Siskiyou Mountains, and I could work the park. Ranger Taggart mentioned an opening. I thought I couldn't work in law enforcement again. I can't take criminals using someone I love against me, but that's happened twice now, and the second time it had nothing at all to do with the fact I was a detective. Because I wasn't. I realized I have no real control over my life."

"I'm sure. I think you would be great as a park ranger, but it sounds like you might be getting ahead of yourself."

"Huh? Oh…" Zach drew in a breath. The moment he'd dreamed of for far too long was upon him. "Marry me, Olivia… Liv, marry me. If you love me."

"Yes, I'll marry you. I can't go through life, I can't go through one more minute, without you by my side as my husband." Olivia leaned in and kissed him.

Clapping resounded from behind. Seemed they had an audience to witness their love.

And God had answered Zach's prayer, this time, the way he had hoped.

* * * * *

Don't miss the other exciting stories
in the WILDERNESS, INC. *miniseries*
by Elizabeth Goddard:

TARGETED FOR MURDER
UNDERCOVER PROTECTOR

Dear Reader,

Thank you so much for reading *False Security*. I hope you enjoyed it! Have you ever been snowmobiling? My husband and I rode snowmobiles on a guided tour through Yellowstone National Park—eighty miles—for one of our anniversaries. It's an exhilarating experience, to be sure. I tried to share some of that exhilaration in my story.

As often happens in novels, there are several themes that run through the story. Readers will usually pick up on one theme that resonates with them. In regards to writing this letter, I selected the theme that resonated with me (in my own story!) in the strongest way.

During the course of writing this, my mom passed away. I couldn't have imagined how difficult it would be to put simple words on paper. I'm thrilled that God answered my prayers and that the required contracted story was produced. But not without a lot of blood, sweat and tears. Adding to my personal loss are many other serious issues I've struggled with the last couple of years.

Of course I pray and sometimes wonder if God hears me. I question His silence or the answers that come in ways I hadn't expected. I realized, too, that I felt so emotionally and psychologically bruised that it was palpable in a very visceral and physical way. Then I pictured myself in a river, fighting to survive and bumping into the rocks and branches and becoming bruised for my efforts.

I had an epiphany at that moment—if I would simply stop fighting that which I could not control, and "go with the flow" as we so often hear—then I wouldn't be so bruised. You might remember reading similar references in the story when Zach thinks of the Rogue River and feels like he's being tossed and twisted in the white-water rapids, being bruised for his efforts to stay alive. He comes to the realization that he should let go and trust God.

So that is the message I hope will resonate with you. Psalm 46:10 in the King James Bible reads "Be still and know that I am God," or as the NASB version translates, "Cease striving and know that I am God."

I pray for His many blessings and favor in your life!

If you haven't signed up for my Great Escapes newsletter, please visit my website today at ElizabethGoddard.com, where you can also connect with me on Facebook and Twitter.

Blessings!
Elizabeth Goddard

The search for a missing colleague puts an FBI agent right in the path of a prison break...and her ex-boyfriend.

Read on for an excerpt from SHERIFF, the next book in the exciting new series ***CLASSIFIED K-9 UNIT.***

The low rumble of a car engine caused FBI agent Julianne Martinez to freeze in her tracks. She quickly gave her K-9 partner, Thunder, the hand signal for "stay." The Big Thicket region of east Texas was densely covered with trees and brush. This particular area of the woods had also been oddly silent.

Until now.

Moving silently, she angled toward the road, sucking in a harsh breath when she caught a glimpse of a black-and-white prison van.

The van abruptly stopped with enough force that it rocked back and forth. Frowning, she edged closer to get a better look.

There was a black SUV sitting diagonally across the road, barricading the way.

Julianne rushed forward. As she pulled out her weapon, she heard a bang and a crash followed by a man tumbling out of the back of the prison van. The large bald guy dressed in prison orange made a beeline toward the SUV.

LISEXP0417

Another man stood in the center of the road pointing a weapon at the van driver.

A prison break!

"Stop!" Julianne pulled her weapon and shot at the gunman. Her aim was true, and the gunman flinched, staggering backward, but didn't go down.

He had to be wearing body armor.

The gunman shot the driver through the windshield, then came running directly at Julianne.

She ducked behind a tree, then took a steadying breath. Julianne eased from one tree to the next as Thunder watched, waiting for her signal.

Crack!

She ducked, feeling the whiz of the bullet as it missed her by a fraction of an inch.

After a long moment, she was about to risk another glance when the gunman popped out from behind a tree.

"Stop right there," he shouted. "Put your hands in the air."

Angry that she hadn't anticipated the gunman's move, Julianne held his gaze.

"Put your hands in the air!" he repeated harshly.

"Fire that gun and I'll plant a bullet between your eyes," a familiar deep husky Texan drawl came from out of nowhere.

Brody Kenner?

Don't miss
SHERIFF by Laura Scott,
available wherever
Love Inspired® Suspense ebooks are sold.